And The Devil Danced!

Janey Clarke

First published in 2025 by Blossom Spring Publishing
And The Devil Danced! (The Devil's Mountain Dames Series)
Copyright © 2025 Janey Clarke
ISBN 978-1-0683266-2-2
E: admin@blossomspringpublishing.com
W: www.blossomspringpublishing.com

Thank you, Lizzie, my wonderful daughter-in-law, who helped plan the original book and the characters of Broken Horseshoe Ranch.

O Lord, God of vengeance,
O God of vengeance, shine forth!
Psalm 94: 1

The avenger of blood shall put the murderer to
death when they meet.

Numbers 35: 21

CHAPTER ONE

"It's a trick! We've been misled again and again with false clues." The suppressed anger in Amy's voice was clear to Josh sitting opposite her. Between them sat an ancient wooden chest. "The chest is empty! It's a rusty, metal-bound box, and it's empty!" The anger and frustration she felt was mirrored in the man's face, who looked devastated at the sight of the empty chest.

Josh stood up and kicked the offending object. "All those symbols! Following every single weird direction and pacing out the exact number. Then we searched for the next carved clue, usually on a precarious rock face! That booby trap in this very cave was meant to kill us. And it nearly did. An avalanche of rocks came down into the entrance and fell into the canyon below. We survived that, and we struggled on through high temperatures, climbed up cliffs, and slid down gullies... And all for nothing! All for an empty chest," Josh shouted.

His face was white with anger and frustration. So many hours of searching through tangles of desert cacti and thornbushes had been spent by the two of them. Up narrow rocky trails to the last clue. Excited, when they realised they had come to the end of their quest. They had dug down into the gravelly soil in the front of a cave, beneath an overhanging rock ledge, in a narrow canyon in the foothills of Devil's Mountain. They had found the chest. Josh had lifted it out, surprised at how light it was. He had placed it in front of Amy, who had helped him dig it out of its hiding place. Their eyes met when he finally forced the rusty metal bands holding the lid down on the box open. Excitement had bubbled up in both of them. Josh threw the lid back. It was empty! "All for nothing, a

1

beautiful, metal-bound chest and it's empty." Josh couldn't contain his fury and strode up and down the rocky ledge outside the cave. The great excitement, which had flared up when they had found the hinged wooden box, evaporated. The disappointment and anger at the empty chest was overwhelming.

"We were told those Jesuits could be tricky. They hid their gold in these mountains. We know that now because we have followed these symbols carved into the rocks to find this. Yes, they were up here, leaving clues for poor fools like us to follow and find it empty. What an inordinate amount of work those Jesuits must have put in just to trick people." His voice spat out the angry words and Josh found himself almost incandescent with rage at the futility of their quest.

Josh Barnes had been found some weeks before unconscious in the desert. There had been no gun, horse, or anything else with him except for a small piece of paper found in his boot. It had said, "*Josh Barnes. Go to Broken Horseshoe Ranch.*" Broad-shouldered, with blonde hair which fell to his shoulders and piercing blue eyes, his long muscular legs made little work of the narrow ledge that he was striding up and down. He stopped for a moment and glanced back at the girl still sitting by the chest.

Amy Tanner had found him that day in the desert. Was it coincidence or fate which had decreed that Amy should be the one to find him? By some fluke, it had been Amy who lived at Broken Horseshoe Ranch and had come across his unconscious body covered in blood. When she had revived him, she brought him home with her to the ranch. Josh watched as she swept a dark auburn braid back over her shoulder. Amy always wore them, tied with twine, hanging down her back. Her pale face never seemed to brown in the sun's rays which so often scorched the desert landscape in which she spent so many hours. Only her freckles seemed to multiply on her face, and when puzzled or laughing, joined up together around her screwed-up, snub nose. Josh felt so deeply about the lack of treasure in the chest because of Amy. Since he'd met her, he'd realised how important the finding of this money was to her. The money would have meant so much to her family.

"Not for nothing! There is something in the chest. Look!" Amy lifted a scroll of parchment, which was hidden in the far depths of the wooden chest. Turning away from the box, she laid the scroll flat on the rock beside her, smoothing it out as she did so.

Josh moved closer beside her, to see over her shoulder. "It's another map. Those Jesuits have left us another treasure chart. Ezra told us they had a name for being cunning and devious. Ezra was correct. This proves it," Amy said.

"Another false trail!" Josh said, determined not to get his hopes up again. "Will this be yet another of those Jesuit tricks? Why should we follow this map!" For a long moment, Josh stared over her shoulder. He didn't know the places mentioned on the map. But at first glance, it looked complicated. The guidelines drawn were meandering throughout the foothills and the peak of Devil's Mountain. "That does not look like an easy map to follow, does it? What do you think, Amy?"

"You're right Josh, it's very complicated. I think Ezra might be the one who could decipher it for us. He's lived in the area for many years, and he knows it well. He knows every inch of the Devil's Mountain." Amy rolled up the parchment and got to her feet. "We found a treasure map, yet another one, Josh. But most important of all, we found a chest after following all those clues. Don't you realise what this means, Josh? Don't you realise that the Jesuit gold exists? We have proved it! Surely, if we follow this map, we will find something at the end of it? They couldn't lead us on a false trail yet again, could they?" Amy's voice and face held hope again. She was putting the disappointment behind her. For Amy, the search had begun again. "Surely this isn't a trick, Josh? Do you think it's another trick?"

CHAPTER TWO

The box was an awkward shape. Rectangular with a barrel-shaped top, it had been fashioned by a craftsman out of dark wood with ornate clasps and hinges. The ancient hinges and lock left their hands rusty red as they struggled to strap it onto Bella's back. "Poor Bella, you have the most unusual things placed upon you, don't you?" Amy said as she patted the gentle horse.

"I should think a small wooden chest is infinitely preferable to a headless body, don't you, Bella?" Josh laughed at the face Amy made at this remark.

Amy's snub nose screwed up, and she shook her head. "Don't remind me! I still have nightmares about that terrible time when we found those headless bodies," Amy shuddered. "Let's get home to the ranch. We haven't found any gold coins, but I think they'll be excited that we have found something. Don't you think that's an achievement, Josh? We have proved that we can follow the clues. All we have to do now is decipher this map and follow the next lot of clues," Amy said as she got on Bella's back. They rode on for a while in silence after these remarks.

Josh looked at the girl riding beside him. Her disappointment had been severe, but as usual, Amy was trying to make the best of it. He hadn't the heart to tell her he thought it was a hopeless cause. What else could he do? "Yes, your father and Ezra will search all over this chart to find out where all the places are mentioned on it. It gives us a new area to search for altogether. I think that will be more interesting. We have been up and down this canyon for quite a time now. I'd like to see somewhere else for a change." Josh had done his best to sound positive, even if he wasn't very enthusiastic about searching again for the elusive Jesuit gold.

"I wonder what Nancy's been doing in our absence. When she suggested marrying my father, I thought it was to enable our lives to carry on as normal. It was to be a marriage of convenience. She would be at Dry Creek Ranch, and we would carry on as usual at Broken Horseshoe Ranch," Amy said.

"Life will never be as usual with Nancy around!" Josh said with a broad grin on his face. His usually solemn face changed, and he looked like a mischievous small boy. "I like Nancy. She might be a bit bossy—"

"A bit bossy! Don't you mean very bossy?" Amy said, turning towards him, a surprised look on her face.

"Okay, she is bossy. But I think she's done wonders with your family. Your father came out here on his doctor's advice to get the desert air in his lungs. What did he do? You have to admit, he tended to sit in the house and mope. It was his choice to buy this ranch because of its proximity to the Devil's Mountain and his dream of finding Jesuit gold. You must see, Amy, that your father is much improved since Nancy came to live at the ranch. Don't you agree with me?"

They rode on in silence for some time. Amy was thinking about what Josh had said. She began biting a nail. Josh hid a smile. Whenever Amy was puzzled or worried or thinking something over, she would bite her nails. Then, realising what she was doing, she almost flung her hand away in disgust. Amy had been seventeen when she had moved out here. An age when a girl should think about parties, new dresses, dancing, and boyfriends. Instead, she found herself living in a basic homestead, comprising a wooden shack with two add-on rooms, each with a dirt floor, and an outside privy. Her bedroom was no bigger than a cupboard, the walls covered with newspaper to keep out the draughts. Another room off this shack was used by Luke, her father, for his bedroom. Ben, her thirteen-year-old brother, slept in a pile of quilts and blankets in a corner of the main room. That corner at night was getting crowded with the influx of Chan, the eleven-year-old Chinese boy, and Josh himself.

"Yes, Josh. You're right, Pa gets so cross with her improvements, and the constant hubbub with the workmen, but it is making him move about more and giving him new interests in life. But Josh, I do know she means well, and she has taken over our family with all our interests at heart and she's so full of good intentions, but is it dreadful of me to find her so irritating?" An anxious frown creased Amy's face, and she looked worried and almost ashamed of her remark.

Josh threw his head back and laughed. "As long as you recognise Nancy's good points, I think it's all right to find her irritating. To be honest, I find her enthusiasm for life wearing myself." They rode on after that in a companionable silence.

"We have two days a week when we are away from the ranch. Tomorrow, we both start work at the general store in Nowhere. I know what you're going to do. You'll be helping Eliza out in the store itself. Manuel says I will help him on his deliveries and his pickups of produce. I don't understand what I have to do. Have you any idea?"

Amy shook her head at this question. "I think there's quite a lot of produce to load and unload from the buggy, and Manuel would like someone with him to help with the heavier loads and for added security. Their son, who usually helped Manuel, is with his grandparents, since his grandmother broke her ankle." Amy turned and looked at Josh and continued speaking. "When I found you in the desert, there was a mark on your trousers from where you had been wearing a gun. Since you've come to the ranch, you've never worn a gun. There have been two attempts on your life, Josh. You've not needed a gun whilst you were safe on the ranch. But you are going out with Manuel around the area and working at the back of the general store. There are lots of strangers around. Any one of them may know you. Since you've lost your memory, you won't recognise them. I think you should take a gun with you, don't you? Manuel has a gun on him at all times. If you are going out with him, there could be attacks. There is always the possibility that the man we heard of as Duke might send someone else to kill you. I think you need to be armed; both for your safety and Manuel's. Don't you think you should carry a gun, Josh?"

"I've never picked up a gun whilst I've been at the ranch. For an excellent reason, Amy. I don't know if I can shoot! What if I can't use a gun anymore? What if I can't shoot a gun?"

CHAPTER THREE

They drew near to the ranch, the wooden box on Bella's back carefully wrapped up in a blanket. In one way, Amy was looking forward to showing the box to her Pa, but the disappointment on his face when he realised it was empty would be hard to bear.

"Every time we go off out somewhere, whenever we return, there's always something going on, with a crowd standing outside the ranch house. Look, what's going on now?" Josh put up a hand to shade his face from the sun and to see more clearly the activity in front of the ranch house.

"It's Nancy again. What is she doing now?" Amy's voice held the usual exasperation she felt at Nancy's constant urge to change everything. She leaned forward, trying to make out the figures clustered around the front porch of Broken Horseshoe Ranch. Then she chewed at a nail.

"She must have another new idea and is explaining it to everyone." Josh swallowed a grin as he saw Amy bite her nail yet again. Nancy and her grand ideas caused considerable flurries to the group living at the ranch. Ben, Amy's younger brother, was always in favour of Nancy's ideas, no matter what she suggested. Chan, the little Chinese boy who now lived with them, always agreed with Ben. Luke, Amy's father who had agreed with this marriage of convenience with Nancy, often just stared at her, gave a large sigh, a shrug of his shoulders, and went back into his bedroom, closing the door firmly behind him. Josh liked Nancy. She had woken up everyone at Broken Horseshoe Ranch, and she always acted with the best of intentions. "You know, if it's Nancy, it will be some new idea for the ranch house, perhaps the introduction of new livestock, or something else to do with the garden."

"Yes, I know Nancy means well. But, Josh, there have been so many changes that Ben and I have had to deal with in such a short time. After the death of our mother, we left our home and the town that we'd grown up in. Then we had another upheaval to come and live here in the foothills of the Devil's Mountain. I think I'm unhappy now about any other changes in my life. I expect you think that's silly of me." Amy's head went down, hiding her expression.

This admission surprised Josh. Amy had never been one to talk about her feelings. She always kept her thoughts to herself. He wondered if it had been because she was so exasperated with Nancy, or was she feeling so at ease with him she could discuss her innermost thoughts with him? Josh knew he had to be careful about what he said in reply. He couldn't laugh off her remark, but he couldn't ignore it. "Amy, I understand. I've lost my memory but have established myself on your ranch, living and working with you all. It's familiar now, and there are no unexpected problems requiring knowledge that I no longer have. So I understand, Amy, how you feel about the changes Nancy is undertaking. I'm not looking forward to going to help at the general store tomorrow. How much of the daily routine at the general store requires knowledge and the background of a normal person that I don't have anymore? Having no memory might make things difficult for me."

They rode on before Amy spoke. "I didn't think, Josh, of how difficult tomorrow may be for you. I know Manuel suspects you in some ways, especially when the masked rider tried to kill you. If we tell Manuel and Eliza the truth about your loss of memory, would that make it easier for you tomorrow?"

Josh thought for a moment, considering her words before he replied. "Yes, Amy, I think it would help. Not only would it help me, but I also don't think it's fair to keep Manuel and Eliza in the dark. They should know the risks attached to having me work for them. Then I wouldn't need to worry about any gaps in my memory if they knew and understood the problem."

"Thank you for listening to me and understanding. I should get used to change in our lives. It will come, no matter what I do." Amy spoke hesitantly. Talking about her feelings was always difficult for her. As she was speaking, they drew nearer to the ranch and could see the group standing outside the ranch house looking up at the stovepipe.

"Yes, Nancy has a new idea," Josh murmured.

"Come and look, you two. Tell me what you think would be best?" Nancy called to them as they dismounted from their horses.

They handed their horses' reins over to Ben and Chan, who always took upon themselves the horses' well-being, taking them to the stable.

"I think the chest will have to wait, don't you?" Josh whispered in Amy's ear as they walked around to join the others. Amy nodded and murmured agreement as she hurried alongside Josh to join the others. Was there a problem? Had her father been ill during the day?

As they approached the group, she heard her father speaking. To her relief, he didn't look ill, but he was annoyed. "I want my coffee good and hot," Luke was protesting.

With his hands on his hips and an irate expression on his face, it was the first time Luke had seemed alive and frustrated since Josh had arrived at the ranch. Whatever plan Nancy had hatched now, Luke was having none of it. Josh folded his arms and drew closer to the group. He was going to enjoy this, whatever the commotion was about.

Nancy grabbed Amy's arm and pulled her to her side, pointing up to the stovepipe jutting out of the cabin roof. "I want that stove and all the cooking and provision stuff out of that room. I want to make it into a sitting room with nobody sleeping in a corner, and no cooking going on in the same space," Nancy said. "What do you think, Amy? Don't you agree with me? We should build a kitchen here and have all the cooking done in it. All your father worries about is his precious coffee being hot! In the heat of the summer, that room is like an oven." Nancy turned and stared at the girl, waiting for her agreement.

"Don't ask me, Nancy. You know well enough that I don't cook. I'm not the person you should be asking. You should ask Leah. She would know what to suggest," Amy said, folding her arms, unwilling to get involved in a disagreement between her father and Nancy.

Whirling around towards the older woman, Nancy practically pounced on her. "Well, Leah, I want your honest opinion. You cook the most delicious evening meals. I know you cook them in your cabin, but a new stove in an outside kitchen would be better. Well, Leah?"

All eyes turned towards the old woman, who flushed at the unwanted attention on her. She smoothed the spotless apron she always wore down with her reddened hands. Her careworn face creased with worry, the wrinkles drawing together in a tight maze of lines. With an encouraging smile from Amy, she drew herself up. "You want me to speak my mind, Mrs Nancy? Are you sure you want to hear what I've got to say?"

"Of course," Nancy said. "I wouldn't have asked you otherwise, would I? Come on, Leah, what do you honestly think?"

CHAPTER FOUR

At Nancy's assurance, Leah began speaking. "Mr Luke needs his coffee all day, every day. It's really good to have that heat in the winter months from the stove. As for adding on a timber room for the kitchen, I think it's a daft idea." Leah paused and looked around, wondering if she should continue. At Luke's beaming smile at these remarks, Leah continued speaking. "I think there should be a covered porch and then a kitchen built, separate from the main cabin. It needs a stove in it, and those cupboards with the screens, if you know what I mean. A basin so that we can always have water would be real handy." The old lady gulped, astonished herself at how she got so many words out in front of everyone.

Silence from everyone made her look around nervously. But it was only because each person who had listened to Leah's speech was considering it. It was Nancy who spoke first. It had to be Nancy, Josh thought to himself.

"That is very sensible, Leah. I agree with everything. The open covered porch between the two dwellings is extremely useful. I've seen them myself in other ranch houses. Yes, that will be the main cookhouse. Your stove in your cabin can keep you warm in the winter, and Luke can still have his everlasting coffee." Nancy clapped her hands. "Right then, let's get to it. How soon can we get this kitchen up and working?"

Murmurs of agreement and nods of approval came from all those standing around.

"Can we have a drink? It's been a long, dusty ride for us to get back to the ranch. Now we've got the kitchen plan sorted, Josh and I would like a drink," Amy said plaintively as she turned away from the group to climb the steps up to the porch, through the door, and straight towards the stove. Grabbing a cloth, she lifted the coffeepot and shook it. It was empty. "Oh dear, I was hoping for a fresh cup the moment I got back."

Chan rushed to take the coffeepot from Amy. "I'll make a fresh pot of coffee for you and Josh."

"Thank you, Chan." Amy smiled at the boy, who was always so eager to please everyone. It had only been a short while since he had been thrown out of the cookhouse belonging to the hotel in Nowhere. The owner, Parker, had bought him from a newspaper advert from back East, worded so it didn't look like a sale but more of a job opportunity. Parker had sent the required amount of payment for a male Chinese worker. It was to Parker's dismay and anger that he discovered he'd bought an eleven-year-old boy when Chan arrived on the scene. Chan was too small to work in the kitchen. He couldn't lift the heavy pots and couldn't cope with the constant rush when serving meals. His arm became dislocated and useless, and he'd been thrown out onto the street by Parker.

Josh and Amy had been shopping at the general store and saw the boy thrown onto the street. Amy had rushed up and paid for the boy, buying him herself. Small for his age, Chan had been covered in burns, cuts, and bruises. Life at Broken Horseshoe Ranch was wonderful for the boy, and he found a new friend in Ben. Helping as much as he could was Chan's goal in life, to show his deep gratitude for his rescue from Parker.

Seated on the porch, coffee in their hands, Josh and Amy had the blanket-wrapped parcel at their feet. Curious eyes had been looking at it, but neither of them spoke about it until both had finished their first cup of coffee.

"What's in the parcel? I carried it from the barn after I got it off Bella's back. It wasn't very heavy. I doubt it's full of gold treasure, is it?" Ben asked, eyeing it hopefully.

Josh looked at Amy. "Shall we put them out of their misery? But we warn you, sadly, there is no gold. But it is an intriguing find we made today." He looked around the porch, checking that only those who knew about Jesuit gold could hear what he was about to say. Luke sat as usual in his rocking chair. The man's eyes were alight with interest, and he leant forward to see better the unwrapping of the parcel. Amy and Nancy were sitting on the bench that sat against the outside wall of the cabin. Ben and Chan were sprawled on the top step of the porch. When there were so many of them on the porch, the chairs from around the table inside were brought out. Josh sat on one chair, the blanket-wrapped object at his feet. He bent over and started unwrapping it.

There were gasps of amazement when the blanket was removed, and the wooden chest was revealed. The rusty, metal-bound box looked out of place on the wooden porch.

"We thought it was empty when we found it," said Amy, and reached into the canvas satchel she always wore across her body. "But we found this inside it. It's some sort of scroll or map." She rose from the bench and handed it to her father.

"Another map? Nothing else in the chest?" Eagerly, Luke held the map with trembling fingers, his excitement obvious as he stared at the map. "No other signs nearby, nothing buried beside it?"

"No, Pa, that was all we found when we dug down. Below that was solid bedrock. There was nothing else besides the chest. Those Jesuits tricked us. All those symbols had us pacing out the right number carved into the rock, and all we found after all that effort was an empty chest." Amy's disappointment was obvious to everyone. Finding the treasure meant so much to Amy. Not for herself: it was for her father and Ben that she longed to find some gold somewhere. Ben was bright and, Amy felt, needed proper schooling – something he was lacking living out in the foothills of the Devil's Mountain. Amy hoped a cure could be found for her father. Surely if they had the right amount of money, someone somewhere would have medicine to make him better?

Josh watched Amy and the expressions flitting across her face. He knew Amy so well now that he understood how much she wanted and needed this money. She didn't want the treasure for herself. That thought had never entered her head. It was all for her father and her brother. But Josh thought that perhaps Amy had got things wrong. There was no cure for her father; no medicine, however expensive, would cure the man. All they could do was give him a healthy lifestyle that would prolong his days before the disease finally took its toll on him. As for Ben, Josh couldn't hide his smile. That boy was loving every moment of living on Broken Horseshoe Ranch. Ben had told him how much he hated school and the rigid lesson plans that didn't interest him. His writing meant everything to him, and the life he was living gave him plenty of material to write about.

"Chan, as you are nearest the chest, can you pass it to me, please?" Luke asked the boy.

Rushing to do Luke's bidding, Chan lifted the chest but hadn't been expecting the awkward shape and weight. He staggered slightly and slipped on the top step. The chest fell out of his hands and crashed down from the top step and on every other step to break at the bottom in smithereens.

Chan fell to his knees, his head in his hands, and wailed. "What have I done? You will send me away now! Don't send me away! Beat me, but don't send me away!"

CHAPTER FIVE

"Don't send me away!" Chan's cries grew louder. He sobbed piteously, and now he was huddled on the floor in a foetal position. "Don't send me away, please."

In seconds, Amy was off the bench and crouching down beside the small boy. She pulled him towards her, took his hands from his face, and wiped the tears from his eyes. "Don't be silly. We won't send you away. It was an accident. We all saw you lose your footing and drop the box." Amy gave him a big hug.

The sobbing lessened. The boy straightened up in the shelter of Amy's arms and looked up at her. He couldn't believe it. His eyes, still full of tears, opened wide. The shuddering body grew still, and he whispered in her ear. "You won't send me away? But I broke the box." Chan gulped and swallowed down the last of his sobs.

Amy smoothed Chan's hair back from the face that was still tear stained and smiled gently. "We won't send you away. It was an accident. And it was only an empty old box." She gave him a kiss and a hug.

Chan stared at Amy, then with a fist, wiped the tears away and threw both arms around Amy, hugging her tightly.

Ben had slipped off the top step on which he had been sitting. He began to put together the broken pieces of the box that had fallen in the dust below the porch. His voice came out in a breathy whisper. "Chan! Reward you, more like. Look at this. Come and see what was hidden in the box!"

Brushing the dust off in quick, excited movements, Ben gathered together all the pieces of the box and rushed up the porch steps and into the cabin. "Quickly! I must sort it all out properly on the table. No one else should see this." The boy looked around to make certain that no one had been watching or listening. "Come on, hurry all of you. Now! Into the cabin immediately!"

Puzzled, yet with growing excitement that had communicated itself from Ben to the others, it took seconds for them all to crowd around the table.

"Close the door. This must be our secret," whispered Ben. First, he laid out across the table the jagged bottom of the box. It had broken into two pieces diagonally. Then the sides followed one after the other, spaced neatly across the table by Ben. The box lid, which had been arched and had some intricate carvings of swirls and circles, had broken straight across, revealing a cavity in each broken segment. Ben took one segment and shook it over the table. Nothing happened. Then, with an excited grin, he said "Watch this." Turning it upside down so that the cavity faced the table, he shook it and a thin wafer of gold slid out, gleaming in the sunlight from the window.

The excited boy held up one of the thin wafers of gold. "You found it, Amy! You've gone and found it. And we'd never have known if Chan hadn't dropped the box." Ben held out a gold wafer to his father after showing it to Amy and Chan.

"I didn't do a bad thing after all? Maybe it turned out good?" Chan whispered, clutching at Amy's skirt and looking at her. "It wasn't a bad thing. The broken box is now good?"

This got another hug from Amy, and she whispered into his ear alone. "Chan, remember this. You are one of the family now. You belong with us."

Josh, who was seated nearby, could hear this whisper, but more importantly, could see Chan's face at these words. Never would he forget the look of wondering joy that spread over the little boy's face as he looked up at Amy, who was sitting on a chair at the table. Chan stared at the girl. "I mean it, Chan, I truly mean it." At these words, the little boy gave a huge gulp and flung his arms around Amy, who hugged him back. As she looked over Chan's shoulder, her eyes met those of Josh. He gave her a sympathetic nod, at which Amy coloured and looked away, but he could tell she was pleased with his approval.

"It is gold!" Luke said, handling it reverently and then passing it to Nancy. "You did it, Amy. You've got onto the track of the Jesuits."

Nancy lifted the broken pieces of wood and stood with them in her hand. "I think these should go in the stove. Amy and Josh, this find of yours must be kept secret. Ben, I am impressed by your presence of mind in bringing this box into the cabin and not shouting out to the world. No one must know of this find, and no one can hear that we're on the track of Jesuit gold. If anyone found out about this, their interest would be intense, and it would bring treasure seekers out of the woodwork, following every movement we made and even digging up the ranch." Nancy walked over to the stove and opened it with one hand. She lifted the pieces of wood and looked at each one of them. "Well? Are you in agreement with me? Luke, I don't think we dare keep it around the cabin, do you?"

"I would have liked to have kept the wood. It would have been interesting to have in my hand an original chest fashioned by the Jesuits themselves. But you're correct, Nancy. They're only broken pieces of wood and dangerous links to the gold to leave lying about the place."

"What about the gold? What are we going to do with that?" Ben held one piece of gold in his hand, smoothing it reverently. "If we take it anywhere... Or try to exchange it for money?"

Luke rose to his feet and held his hand out for the gold wafer Ben still held. It was given to him, reluctantly. Ben had his eyes fixed on the gold and did not want to part from it. "Quite right, Ben. Let's hide this away until we need it desperately. Then it can be taken to a town where no one knows us and can be exchanged for cash." The two wafers of gold now sat in Luke's hand. His eyes – faded now with the illness and age – were full of tears of joy and happiness. A dream, based on a trusted friend's map and a Spanish coin, that had seemed impossible to achieve, had become a reality and was sitting in the palm of his hand. "It should be hidden, then we have it whenever we need it. This is a hard life we lead out here in the West. Unexpected needs arise and it would be a wonderful nest egg to fall back on. Is everyone agreed on this? Ezra built this log cabin with the former owner. They have built-in, secret places. Hidden to sight, they are ideal for securing items of value. There's one in my bedroom. I'll go in and secure the gold there now." Luke paused at the door of his bedroom and looked back at them, awaiting any disagreement with his plan. Nods of approval greeted his speech. It was the best way they all felt to keep themselves and the gold safe and secure.

Ben jumped to his feet. "I'm hungry. I'm going to see if Leah has dinner ready. Coming, Chan?" Josh and Amy followed Ben out onto the porch. Ben ran round to the cabin behind them, from where they could smell Leah's cooking drifting towards them in the evening breeze.

"Now I can smell cooking, I'm hungry too. Are you

hungry, Chan?" Josh, who had reached the bottom step of the porch, turned to face the young boy who was standing on the top step. Chan threw himself at Josh, who opened his arms wide to catch the boy. "Whoa, there, Chan. What's all this about?"

The skinny body was light for Josh to catch. The boy's arms went round his neck and clung to him. "Thank you, Josh. You and Miss Amy rescued me. Thank you, Josh." The unexpected hug from the boy brought a lump to Josh's throat. He held the boy away and whispered to him. "You were worth rescuing, Chan. It's great to have you here with us." And he swung the boy around, making him shriek with laughter, before putting him down and sending him off after Ben.

Amy and Josh exchanged glances and laughed with each other. No words were necessary. Both knew what the other was thinking.

"I'll get the table ready for dinner," and Amy went back into the cabin.

Josh was about to join her in the cabin, but he stopped with one foot in midair above the second step. Hairs were rising on the back of his neck. Josh knew that feeling. There was no mistaking it. Someone was watching him!

CHAPTER SIX

Josh turned around, slowly searching for any movement or figure. Nothing. The feeling persisted, and Josh tried to work out what exactly he was experiencing. He knew he was the focus of somebody's eyes. That he was certain of. It was an instinctive feeling, but there was no malice in the gaze upon him. Whoever was watching him meant him no harm.

Amy came out onto the porch and touched Josh on the arm. "Come in, Josh, you'd better hurry. Ben and Chan are eating everything in sight. There will be nothing left for us." Amy must have seen the expression on Josh's face. "What's the matter?" she asked him. He looked at her, shook his head slightly, and indicated that they should stay outside on the porch before the others heard his remarks.

"Someone was watching me. I felt it again." Josh looked around the ranch as if the watcher would suddenly jump up and wave at him.

On hearing these words from Josh, Amy paled and looked nervously around. "Do you think someone is out to kill you again? Do you think it's another of the men hired by the man the masked rider called Duke?" Amy had lowered her voice so that the others inside would not hear her anxious questioning. "We would have seen or heard someone on horseback if they came near to the ranch." Her gaze swept the horizon around the ranch, but like Josh, she could see nothing.

"This time there was no feeling of evil coming from whoever was watching me. Not like before. The scrutiny by the masked rider was accompanied by the most overwhelming feeling of malice and animosity. This time

I felt curiosity, that's all." Josh looked down at the girl beside him. Her face was serious, and she put a hand up to her face and began nibbling her nail. "Do you think I imagined it? Am I getting paranoid, expecting people to be everywhere I am, waiting to shoot me?" His question came out with a harshness that showed his feeling of being powerless against not only the man who was conspiring with others to kill him but also his blank memory, which was also betraying him. His face was now set in hard lines, his jaw clenched in impotent anger. Josh ran a hand through his overlong blonde hair, leaving it in a tousled mess. "Who is watching me now? Why can't I remember who wishes me harm?"

There was silence for a moment as Amy thought about his words. Again, she touched him on the arm, this time with sympathy for his plight. "No, Josh, I don't think you're imagining it at all. You may have lost your memory, but you haven't lost the senses you had before. In fact, I should think they're more powerful now. Your increased need to survive may well have sharpened your ability to sense danger. At least you felt no hate coming towards you this time." Her hand dropped to her pocket, and he could tell that she was holding the knife that she always kept there within easy reach. Josh remembered that knife and how it had saved their lives a few days ago. "It just proves that we have to remain vigilant, Josh. We can't drop our guard for a single minute." With a last look and another fruitless gaze around the ranch, they left the porch.

After the meal, the evening was spent examining the scroll on which the map had been drawn, that had been found in the chest. They compared it with the map that Luke had brought out with him, and the map Ezra had received from the dying Mexican.

"It's in a completely new direction from all the other maps I've ever seen," said Ezra. "It's on the other side of Devil's Mountain, far away from the rocky foothills of the mountain itself. Look," an aged, knobbly finger pointed to the map. "This map leads around the mountain and down to the south. That's Lonesome Creek along there. It's not the sparse desert land you've been searching over. It's got trees and bushes, and along the creek bed itself, there are boulders piled high, and thick scrub vegetation that makes the going almost impossible." Ezra sat back in his chair and looked at Josh and Amy. "That desert land you've been searching through is hard enough, but this is more difficult in yet another way. It's so easy to get lost there in all the tangles of shrubs, bushes, trees and cacti. Most of the bushes have spiteful thorns, and there are plenty of snakes, insects, and critters hidden in amongst the undergrowth."

With Ezra's gloomy predictions ringing in their ears, they all went to bed. Josh thought he would sleep that night after the day's excitement, but he tossed and turned. He would dearly have loved to get up and pace the floor but sharing the quilts and mattresses with the two boys, it was impossible. There was no way he wanted to wake them up. Time enough to see them and listen to their incessant chatter in the morning.

He thought back to earlier that evening when they had taken him out to Ben's target practice area. A plank of wood had been set up for Ben to improve his sharpshooting. His prowess after his constant practice was considerable as he hit the lopsided face and body drawn on the plank of wood time and again.

Nancy had produced a large bag and handed it to Josh.

"Belonged to my late husband. You'll find his guns and some of his coats in there. Be pleased if you could find a use for them." The gruff voice showed how important it was to Nancy that Josh accept her gift. Josh did with gratitude. There was no need to hide his delight. She could see it in his face. His thanks were profuse as he strapped on the gun and holster. Both were of superb quality and the coats fitted him well, if a little baggy around his middle.

Luke had joined the group and was watching as Josh stood, uncomfortably aware of the many eyes upon him. The unfamiliar feel of the gun and holster made him nervous, and the target seemed to move further away each time he looked at it.

"Josh, close your eyes. Feel the gun and remember where the target was. When I say shoot, open your eyes and do that immediately. There will be an automatic muscle reaction you will have had if you shoot regularly." Luke told him and gave the nervous Josh a smiling nod of encouragement.

"Here goes! I'm ready, Luke." Josh stood straighter, pulling his shoulders back and letting his hand hover over the gun. His eyes were tightly closed.

"Shoot!" Luke shouted.

CHAPTER SEVEN

The shot rang out and the lopsided face had another hole in it, right through the nose.

"Great shooting Josh! Try again," Luke said. The others around Josh gave a cheer and, with renewed confidence, he put the gun back in its holster, ready for his next shot.

"Let me shout shoot," Ben cried out, rushing towards Josh.

"Don't close your eyes this time, Josh. Look and aim at the target," was Ezra's advice.

Later, when the night shadows were darkening, and it was becoming too difficult for Josh or anyone else to see the target, Josh was elated. He walked back into the cabin, feeling the reassuring presence of the gun on his hip. Luke had been right. It had all come back automatically to him. He could shoot again and defend himself. With that comforting thought, he drifted off to sleep.

The next morning, Amy and Josh rode to Nowhere to start their new jobs at the general store. Josh was wearing a blue flannel shirt and a heavy canvas jacket, both of which had belonged to Nancy's husband. They fitted him well, and he felt better in them and was eager to begin his new position with Manuel. The gun sat snugly in its holster, a reassuring presence on his hip.

"I wonder how they will react to your admission of losing your memory and having killers after you?" Amy asked Josh. They had discussed it at length over breakfast. And it had been agreed by everyone present that the truth about Josh had to be told to Manuel and Eliza. "I know them only from getting provisions at their store. I don't know if they will understand and accept us. We may have to turn round and go back to the ranch," Amy said.

"We tell them immediately we walk in that store," Josh said, as they took their horses round the back of the general store and into the small stable Manuel had for his horses. They both lingered over settling the horses down. Neither wanted to explain Josh's difficult situation.

They needn't have bothered worrying. Manuel and Eliza were shrewd enough to have realised that there were problems concerning Josh's background. Having worked with people, and catering to the mixed assortment of customers they had to deal with daily, the couple didn't take long to make up their minds about people.

"We've known Ezra over many years, and we respect Luke's judgement. They both vouch for you and so we will have you working for us, as agreed," Manuel said, with Eliza nodding in the background.

"Let's get to it, Josh. You'll help me load up the wagon, ready to go out to a couple of ranches. They have a usual weekly order, and I have goods from them in return to sell in the shop." After they loaded up the wagon, Manuel turned to Josh. "I must go to the saloon. The Grangers always ask me to bring whiskey and beer for them. I don't stock alcohol, but I always get it from the saloon for customers when I deliver. Come on, it's been hot, dusty work. I think we deserve a beer."

Manuel led the way across Main Street to the saloon. It was just as Josh remembered from his first and only visit there. The wooden front hid the tent saloon behind. Pushing through the swing doors, Josh was hit by the smell. There was a pungent smell of unwashed bodies, which fought with the smell of the beer. Overriding all other smells was the smoke from cigars and handmade cigarettes which lingered in the corners of the tent and hung in the air. A large table, which was used as a bar, was at the back of the tent. Round, rough-hewn tables stood in the centre of the tent with a few stools at each one. In front of the bar, there were some stools on which three men were sitting. Slumped in a corner was an older man who, to Josh's eyes, looked as if he'd been there all night. Outside the tent and behind the bar was a wooden shed-like structure with a large padlock. Seth, the saloon owner, and Manuel went into it to get the required order for Manuel to deliver. Josh reckoned it was where Seth stored all his supplies. Looking at the rough crowd in the tent, that padlock was essential.

"What do you want?" A thin-featured man with a droopy moustache was wiping down the tables and serving. When finished with one customer, he came over to Josh. A soiled apron was wrapped around his scrawny body. Covered in so many stains, it no longer had any trace of the original white. "Well, what do you want?" He repeated, glaring at Josh.

"Two beers," Josh replied, ordering one for himself and one for Manuel. He took the two bottles, then stood at the end of the bar cum table, waiting for Manuel.

Josh hadn't been conscious of the three men who were already seated when he entered. But they had been watching him.

"Whining dog of an Englishman, ain't you?" The man nearest to Josh had turned around on his stool, all the better to insult him.

Josh looked at the man, and taking his time, really looked at all three of them. His initial thoughts were that they could all do with a good wash. They were dirty, dishevelled, and reeking of many days' journeys with no thought of washing themselves. The one nearest to him had a scar across his face, from forehead to chin. His greying whiskers and hair were matted, and the sneering smile showed a lack of teeth.

"Yellow dogs, all those English. You look yellow through and through." Again the sneering remark, which made his two companions roar with laughter and slap their thighs in merriment.

Josh was taken aback. The discomfort he felt at this verbal attack upon him was compounded by his blank memory. What did he do in this situation? He couldn't remember. Surely he must have had some sort of routine reply or... What did he do then? And what was he going to do now?

CHAPTER EIGHT

Whilst Josh was thinking things through, the scarred guy had risen to his feet and was standing threateningly. Of a similar height to Josh, he was broader and carried himself with a swagger, clenching and unclenching his fists provocatively.

"Go on, Abe, you show him. We don't want no English down here." One of his companions thumped him on the back and pushed him forward towards Josh.

Abe ran towards Josh and raised his fists. "I'm going to show you what Americans are made of!" He threw a punch at Josh. The fist that flew towards Josh's head was scarred and meaty and moved fast.

Like a flash, Luke's words from last night darted into Josh's brain. "Remember, Josh, your brain might not remember, but your body and muscles keep the memory of previous actions. Rely on your body's memory." Josh, in that fleeting second, relaxed his brain and let fly with a series of punches that knocked the man down onto the floor. Gasping, Abe floundered on the floor, blood gushing from his nose, which was broken, and by the look of it, Josh thought, not for the first time.

"You were saying?" Josh said, looking down at the man, and shaking his hand, which was now hurting after the blows he had rained on his attacker. "We can see now what you are made of. There's enough blood on the floor."

Manuel had returned with Seth, both carrying bottles and boxes for Manuel's delivery to the Grangers' ranch. Both were horrified at the sudden eruption of a fight when they had only turned their backs for a moment.

"Out of it, you three. You've been sitting here nursing

one drink for long enough. Now you attack a paying customer. Go on, clear off." Seth reached under the table for a large piece of timber. He lifted it, then slapped it into his hand. It gave a satisfying *thunk* as it hit his palm. Seth was a burly man, although running to fat and getting on in years. But his determined look and the muscular arms that were holding the wood made the three drifters think again.

The two that were still standing hoisted up their friend and helped him out of the door. But not before the bloody man muttered imprecations under his breath at Josh. "I'll get you, English! I'll make you sorry for this. You see if I don't!"

Seth reappeared behind the bar and pushed Josh's beer towards him across the counter. "There was some science behind those punches. You knew what you were doing, Josh. Those three meant trouble the moment they walked into the bar. They were looking to pick a fight with anyone. It just happened to be you. Come on now, drink up, you deserve it."

It was only a few moments later that Josh and Manuel, carrying the Grangers' orders for alcohol, placed them in the waggon, along with the rest of the day's deliveries. The long day was hot, and their arrival at each new ranch was greeted with a very different welcome. The first two ranches were small and close to one another, and Manuel explained the owners were two brothers who worked together, supporting each other in all they did. One brother met them with his latest batch of eggs and three chickens which squawked unhappily as they were placed in a basket in the waggon. The brother said hello to them, and goodbye, and that was all. Josh was aware of the figures peeking out at them from behind a tree and from the cabin itself.

"The others that live here, don't they ever speak or come out to see you?" Josh asked Manuel as they fixed the chickens in a more secure place, which also happened to move their constant noise further away from their ears.

"No, it's only the one brother, and he says nothing. They order the same provisions each week, but the provisions they give me in return vary. Each quarter I add it all up, having written it down each week, and with the brother agree payment if needed. It usually works out that there's nothing to pay on either side."

They set off once more, Josh becoming interested in the characters he met. They all tried to make a living and carve out a life for themselves in this desolate landscape, fighting against the desert itself, let alone the harsh weather, the loneliness, and, of course, the Indians.

"Now we go on to the Grangers. They are a different type of rancher. They came here some time ago with money in their pockets, some knowledge of ranching, and the ability to cope with the unexpected hazards of life here," Manuel told Josh as they drove on until they finally reached the sign that just said, *"The Grangers"*. They rode up to the ranch house, and Josh was amazed to find a garden in front of it. He felt certain that his mouth had dropped open, and that he just could not stop staring.

"An astonishing sight, isn't it?" Manuel chuckled at Josh's face. "Mrs Granger is most insistent on having some flowers outside her front door. I think she'd deprive the whole ranch, including everyone working on it and her husband, of water, just to make sure her flowers survived. I don't know why they moved out here. Can't understand it, moving here when you have money to spare. Who'd want to eke a living out here if you didn't have to?"

Josh went round to the back of the wagon to help Manuel as they began unloading.

Rushing down the porch steps, a worried man began shouting to Manuel excitedly. Behind him, a woman stood wringing her hands again and again. "Manuel! Manuel, we've had a visit from Shadowhawk. Do you know if anyone else has had a break-in to their properties in Nowhere or around it? No one heard or saw him come into the house."

"How do you know it was Shadowhawk?" Manuel asked Mr Granger, as he carried one box up the porch steps. He halted in front of the flustered man.

"Look, Manuel! Look at this. It's a hawk feather! This proves it was Shadowhawk. Why did he break in here?"

CHAPTER NINE

Manuel and Josh stood on the porch surrounding the Grangers' ranch house. The property was well cared for and large compared to the Broken Horseshoe Ranch. Josh couldn't help but contrast the grand surroundings the Grangers lived in and the broken down cabin of the Tanners.

"We found it this morning on the table. The front door was open and nothing had been taken," Mr Granger said, putting an arm around his wife, who was shaken by the entire experience. A small, dumpy woman, she looked up to her husband, hanging on to his every word with admiration. He was a large, bluff mountain of a man. His red face beamed joviality, or as Josh thought, perhaps it showed his liking for alcohol. But he was kind enough to insist they both sit down and have a cup of coffee while he told them all about the intruder.

The large room, with its views over the garden and the Devil's Mountain beyond, was furnished with style and exceptionally comfortable chairs. Josh sank into one and felt the tense muscles in his body relax. Coffee was brought into them by a smiling Mexican woman, along with biscuits and dainty cakes. Manuel and Josh enjoyed every bite and neither of them refused coffee refills. It was an excellent blend of freshly ground coffee.

Mr Granger continued his story. "There was nothing obvious to see, except that the front door was left open, and the large feather was placed in the centre of our kitchen table. There was also this paper with the Bible verses on it."

The feather was left on the table, but he passed the verses to Manuel, who passed it on to Josh.

O Lord, God of vengeance,
O God of vengeance, shine forth!   Psalm 94: 1.
The avenger of blood shall put the murderer to death
when they meet.
Numbers 35: 21.

"What can it mean? Who breaks into a house and leaves Bible verses?" The older man shook his head as Josh passed the paper back to him. Both Manuel and Josh, having looked at the paper and read the Bible verses, were equally at a loss. Neither of them knew what to say, but luckily, Mrs Granger spoke.

"But remember, dear, the papers that were strewn all over your desk and on the floor," Mrs Granger reminded her husband.

"Of course. How could I forget that? Whoever it was didn't come to steal anything, but went through all our personal papers. They were searching for something. Whatever it was, they didn't find it, and just left everything everywhere. But there was no damage. Nothing broken and nothing stolen." Mr Granger took a large swallow of his coffee, placing his mug on the table.

Josh caught him eyeing the large box that they had placed on a table on the porch through the open door. Mrs Granger had already removed all the provisions and the perishables, taking them into the kitchen, Josh suspected. But the box standing beside the table contained many bottles of beer and a couple of bottles of whiskey. Josh thought to himself that as soon as they left the Grangers' ranch house, one of those bottles would definitely be opened. As Mr Granger's eagle eye rested again on the whiskey bottle, he felt certain that Mr Granger's next mug of coffee would be topped up by some whiskey.

When they left, after hearing the tale of Shadowhawk several times over, they had added to their store of provisions some butter, eggs, and a few large cakes made by Mrs Granger.

Manuel assured Josh that the cakes were eagerly sought after in his store. "These are her coffee cakes. Eliza and I always have one for ourselves." Manuel placed them in the waggon with the greatest care, even more so than when he handled the eggs. "Take one back with you tonight. I'm sure it will be welcomed by Luke, even if his appetite is poor."

"What do you make of this tale about Shadowhawk, Josh?" Manuel asked him. They had been driving along for some time, and the heat of the day was getting intense, the sun now overhead. Neither had felt like a conversation as they suffered the hot, dusty journey.

"I don't understand it at all. A burglar who breaks into people's houses to read their private papers. It's unbelievable that anyone should go to all this trouble. What can be his motive? What is this Shadowhawk looking for? And why leave a hawk feather?" Josh posed the questions, but could not think of any answers. "It's the Bible verses I find so puzzling. Vengeance seems to be the message that the burglar has left behind. Vengeance by whom? And what crime needs avenging?"

Manuel pushed his belly into a better position over his trousers, gave it a scratching in passing, and said thoughtfully, "By all accounts, this burglar got in and out without them being any the wiser. If that was the case, why show that you've been in the homestead? Why leave a mess of papers and that hawk feather?" Manuel shook his head. "It's getting too hot to think properly. Let's think about this later. Only got to go to the Widow

Perkins' house and then we go back to the store."

"Dry Creek Ranch? Nancy's place? But she's living over at Broken Horseshoe Ranch now." A surprised Josh turned to look at Manuel.

"Just because she's living with you lot, doesn't mean they don't eat over there. Miguel has a large family to feed, and, of course, there are the ranch hands on the property. He's a pretty fine gardener and often has lots of produce for me to sell in the store. But they have little water, not like you at Broken Horseshoe. Nancy's got big ideas in the gardening produce line for your place," Manuel told Josh.

Josh had helped Manuel unload all the produce and provisions they had collected on their deliveries. It wasn't an onerous job, but Josh appreciated how much faster it was with the two of them working together. It must have taken Manuel a long time on his own.

The coffee cake was placed with great care in the back of the buggy. Josh was standing by the buggy with Bella when Amy came out of the store. She smiled at him. Manuel had locked up the stable for the night, waved Amy off, and then locked the door behind her. The stable yard had dark pools of shadow, which lengthened as the sun began dipping over the horizon. With the normal daily bustle of the general store no longer there, it had become eerily quiet.

Amy walked towards Josh and the buggy with a cheerful smile on her face. "How was your day, Josh? I enjoyed helping Eliza."

A burly man emerged from the shadows. "Move aside, little Missy. I'm going to teach this Englishman a lesson!" Abe said. He walked towards Amy and shoved her from behind, catching her unawares. She hurtled forward, caught off balance, only breaking her fall by catching on to Bella.

"I think we'll have a little fun with him first, don't you, fellas?"

Another two figures, laughing and with fists raised, stepped out of the shadows to join Abe. They moved towards Josh and circled him, cutting off any chance of escape.

"No one punches Abe and gets away with it. I told you that you'd regret it. We're going to make sure you do!"

CHAPTER TEN

They ignored Amy, who struggled to regain her balance. They walked past her towards Josh. Amy, meanwhile, had righted herself, crept forward behind Bella and the buggy, and now stood behind them as they drew nearer to Josh.

"I don't think so." Amy stepped out from behind Bella with her Peacemaker in her hand.

"Well, look here. This little lady has a gun. Careful, you don't hurt yourself." Abe, with his broken nose, still swollen and still smeared with blood, slapped his hand on his thigh and laughed uproariously. The others laughed with him. "Don't you frighten yourself when it goes bang!" Abe laughed again.

"Now then, we didn't reckon on no shooting. We only wanted to rough him up a bit. Maybe break his nose, and a few more bones besides." Laughter erupted from the men as they drew ever nearer to Josh in a tightening circle.

Josh stood his ground. His hands were clenched at his sides. He was also conscious of the reassurance of the gun in its holster at his hip. But he didn't want to use his gun. There were too many of them, and he'd never survive, nor would Amy. "Go back to the saloon. There's no need for any trouble. We're going home. We've been working hard all day, and we don't want any nonsense now," Josh tried to reason with the men.

That made the men laugh even more. "My, listen to him! He doesn't want any nonsense. Doesn't he speak nicely?" It was obvious to Josh that they had returned to the saloon after his fight with Abe and had probably spent the afternoon drinking there. They were in that state of recklessness only a copious amount of drink can produce. Josh didn't want a gunfight, not here in a confined space between the small stables in the back of Manuel's store. Somehow, he knew that bullets in such a confined space could ricochet and cause problems no matter where you stood. And there was Amy: it was the last thing he wanted, to see her hurt, or even killed, because of his English accent.

"You mean to fight with me because I speak with a funny accent?" Josh couldn't believe that. It was just so ridiculous.

"I don't like the way you talk, and I don't like the way you punched my nose! You gotta pay for that, Limey. Me and my friends are just gonna show you how we punch." The three of them moved nearer to Josh. Abe wiped his bloody nose with his hand. He looked down at the blood-smeared knuckles and swore loudly before rushing towards Josh.

"I don't think so!" Neither Josh nor the three men had noticed that Amy had slipped round the back of the buggy past Bella and come out behind the three men. "If you don't leave this yard , now, I'll start shooting. I can't decide which one of you to shoot first. Where should I shoot you? Perhaps only in an ankle? Or an arm? I think the best idea is for you all to get going before I make up my mind." Amy stood ready to fire her Peacemaker, pointing it at the central figure, at Abe.

Abe turned and laughed at her. "Careful now, little girl, that gun makes a nasty bang." He repeated the words, again with a coarse, braying laugh, thinking them clever and amusing. Again, he slapped his thighs, encouraging his friends to join in with his laughter.

They didn't. Perhaps they hadn't had as much to drink

as he had. Both of them saw the determination in Amy's face, the set of her jaw, and her firm lips tightly pressed together. They realised not only that the hand holding the Peacemaker was steady and aiming at the leader's ankles, but also that it looked as if she knew what she was doing. They shook their heads and took to their heels.

Placing his hands on his hips, Abe stood his ground and sneered at Amy. "You wouldn't dare shoot and..."

Amy shot the toe off his boot. He jumped back, swearing at her.

"If you don't leave now, it won't be the toe of your boot, it will be your ankle." She aimed the gun at his foot and slowly moved it up towards his ankle.

With a torrent of abuse aimed at her, he half ran, half staggered out of the yard. The sole of his boot flapped with every step he took. Josh watched him leave, and then asked Amy, "Would you have shot him in the ankle?"

Amy replaced the gun in her holster and looked up at Josh. "Yes, I would have. Those men were drunk and had no qualms about beating you up and attacking me, just for fun. If shots were fired, by them or us, or I screamed loud enough, it could have escalated. Manuel and Eliza could have been caught in the crossfire. Shooting him in the ankle would be a small price for him to pay to save everyone else a lot of bother."

"I didn't draw out my gun, I was frightened it would..." Josh began speaking.

Amy climbed into the buggy. "They'd have drawn their guns and killed you then and there. You did the right thing, Josh. Now, can we get home? Serving in that shop all day was tiring. Aren't you tired after helping Manuel?"

Josh climbed up beside her as Amy spoke to Bella and picked up the reins, driving the buggy out of Manuel's yard. They had been fortunate that the one shot Amy had fired had alerted no one else in Nowhere. They drove off as the sun was setting, eager to return home. It was later that Josh voiced his thoughts. "Do you think those men will hang around Nowhere and look for more trouble with me?"

"No, I don't think so. I hope not. From what I heard in the store today, they were drifters heading for the mines and going to prospect for silver. I heard today there's been a large amount of silver found over by the Avon River. I only hope they set off soon and leave us in peace," Amy replied.

"They don't look like miners. I don't see them putting in any hard work digging up the gold or silver. I can see them robbing miners though," said Josh.

They approached the ranch, and Josh raised himself to see the ranch house.

"What is it, Josh? Is there a problem at the ranch?" Amy screwed up her eyes, holding her hand up to shield them from the sun, trying to see what had interested Josh. "What is it, Josh? What's happening there now? Is there something wrong at the ranch? What are you looking at, Josh?"

CHAPTER ELEVEN

Josh smiled at Amy. "Nothing! I see nothing at all. There is no one. There is no Nancy with a crowd of people around her. It's all right Amy, I think that we have managed to arrive home for once without Nancy causing a hubbub." Josh grinned at her. "I'm sorry. I just couldn't resist it." His blue eyes were sparkling and crinkling at the corners as his smile changed his normally solemn face into that of a carefree young man.

"Josh Barnes! You were teasing me, weren't you?" Amy turned to look at him, and then she punched him in the arm with all her strength. "You had me worried. That wasn't fair." Her voice was angry, but her eyes laughed with him. A shared look of amusement passed between them.

"Sorry, Amy, I just couldn't resist it. You looked so worried at the thought of Nancy up to her tricks again," Josh said, as he rubbed his shoulder. "Do you know you pack quite a punch?"

They drew up to the ranch, and the cabin door opened. Ben and Chan dashed down the steps to greet them. "We'll do the horses and then bring dinner in. Wait till we come back in to tell us all the news. We don't want to miss any of it. You will wait for us, won't you?" Ben said as he reached up to take the horses.

The entire group at the Broken Horseshoe Ranch enjoyed hearing about the day's events at the general store. Over dinner, Josh and Amy recounted the day's events, but both of them left out the trouble they had had with Abe. Luke would only have worried and might have refused to let Amy return to help Eliza out at the general store. It was an interesting evening because Nancy

45

listened quietly and said very little. Josh wondered what was worrying her. Or perhaps she had some new idea for livening up Broken Horseshoe Ranch yet further and was wondering what their reaction would be.

Amy was yawning soon after her meal. The unexpected happenings of the day, together with the work and new experiences involving the general store, had left her tired. She soon went to bed, leaving the others still chatting. Finally, Nancy and the boys, realising how tired Josh was, also went to bed.

Security around the ranch had been stepped up since the advent of Shadowhawk. A large wooden bar was placed across the front door of the cabin now, as well as having the windows shuttered each night. The sleeping arrangements were still such that only Luke could go to bed when he wanted. The others had to go to bed all at the same time.

They were all awoken the next morning by the urgent sound of knocking and banging on the door. "Wake up! Let me in! You must come and see this!"

It was Ben who reached the bar first, lifting it and throwing it on the floor, then opening the door wide.

Leah rushed into the cabin, her hair (usually so tidy) sticking up in all directions, and she looked more puzzled than frightened. "It's the third day running. I went out to milk the cow, and somebody's been there before me. I thought I was imagining it the last few days... And not only that, but some eggs have also been taken."

At her excited exclamations, Ezra, who had followed her in, said, "Leah is correct, there are drips of milk on the ground." He was also worried and upset by his wife's unusual findings that morning. Nancy appeared from the cupboard bedroom she still shared with Amy, her hair hanging loose down her back. Amy followed, still with one bare foot, one sock clutched in her hand.

"And..." Looking around at the eager audience she now had waiting for her next remarks, Leah drew a deep breath. "And that rough ground, next to the vegetable garden, that we were going to dig next has been cleared of stones and is now dug over, ready for planting!"

These remarks set off a stampede. Ben and Chan were first out the door. They ran over to the vegetable garden and stood staring at all the neatly turned ground. Following hard on their heels was Nancy, her wild grey hair flowing in the wind, and then Josh and Amy. Struggling to put her sock on one foot as she hopped along, Amy grabbed hold of Josh's arm to steady herself as they arrived to join the others.

"That was going to be our job today, Chan. I don't think we'd have done it as good as this, do you?" Ben said as he admired the newly tilled earth.

"I know you wouldn't have done it that well, and you would have moaned the entire way through it," Nancy said, staring down at the earth. "I don't understand. Who would come along in the middle of the night, steal eggs and milk, and then dig the garden? It can't be the Shadowhawk, can it?" Nancy looked round at the others, hoping that they might have the answer.

"Have we had a visit from Shadowhawk? Do you think it was Shadowhawk?"

CHAPTER TWELVE

No one knew if it had been Shadowhawk or not. Never had a patch of newly dug earth been more scrutinised and commented upon. Shaking their heads, they all walked back to the ranch to get organised for the day ahead.

"We'd better hurry. We can't be late for Manuel," Josh said as they entered the cabin again. "Are you nearly ready, Amy?"

"Yes, I'll just take Pa his morning cup of coffee before I go. Ben, can you pour one out for Pa and one for me and Josh?"

"Josh and Amy, don't you want breakfast? Can I get you something?" Chan asked them both as he stood with a skillet in his hand and a worried expression on his face. It was Chan who made breakfast every morning, and he became most upset if it wasn't wanted. Luke remained in his room with only a coffee each morning until he felt stronger and able to face the day ahead.

At yet another anxious query from Chan, Josh relented and said to the boy, "Can you do something for us to eat on the way to the general store? Could you manage that for us, Chan?"

The eager young boy dashed over to the stove and began banging pots, pans, and plates with a cheerful smile on his face.

When Amy came out of her father's room, she looked solemn and unhappy. Josh knew her father was not getting any stronger, but was losing ground against the disease that held such a tight grip on his lungs. "I'm ready, we'd best get going now, Josh."

"Here you are. There is bread, cheese, and bacon, all wrapped up in the cloth for you."

"Thank you, Chan, that is so good of you. I'm hungry and I don't want to serve behind the counter with a grumbling tummy," Amy said to the young boy, who giggled at that remark.

At the general store, the morning deliveries passed quickly, and Josh soon got in the way of it with Manuel. He could see that the older man was delighted with the help he could give him and that the journeys and deliveries went much quicker with the two of them. Josh wondered if the companionship they shared, as well as the added security, were as important to Manuel as the help with the heavier loads.

As for Amy, she too settled into Eliza's rhythm in the store. She helped sort out the vegetables, checking in case any had gone bad or looked damaged. Some were put on one side for Manuel and Eliza to use up themselves, and others were placed in a special basket to be sold at a much cheaper price than the good ones. The customers coming in expressed surprise at seeing her work there. Most of them chatted with her, smiled, and exchanged pleasantries. A few did not wish to talk, even with Eliza, but bought their necessities and then scurried away.

"We haven't had the gossips in yet. Wait till you meet them, Amy," Eliza said. She was straightening the fabrics she had ordered and placing them to their best advantage at the back of the shop. Alongside them, Eliza had sent away to the merchants in the nearest town for all the necessities that most of the women needed for everyday sewing. Most ladies living out in frontier towns made their clothes and their menfolk's clothes and generally took care of all the household linens. Eliza was a shrewd businesswoman, and she had seen, in the growth of the small township and the influx of more women joining their husbands, a chance to earn money from pretty accessories.

"Let's open this box that came in from the merchant yesterday, Amy. I didn't have time yesterday, and I knew you would love to see what's in it. Manuel thinks I'm being silly, he knows how difficult it is around here for people to feed and clothe themselves, but I thought these, which are reasonably priced, would be enjoyed by the ladies." The string was cut, and the brown paper was taken off and folded neatly for further use. Then Eliza opened the box and placed the objects within it on the wooden counter.

"Oh, how lovely! I think these are so pretty. Are they very expensive?" Amy asked, touching the pretty buttons, the coloured satin ribbons, and the embroidery threads.

The door opened, and both women turned to greet the newcomer. A striking young woman stood there, dressed in sober colours: a dark burgundy costume over which she wore a matching mantle. Her coal-black hair was pulled back into a neat bun. The woman looked round the store and then came towards them both and stood at the counter. "Good morning, I have just arrived here and I'm staying at the hotel whilst I await the arrival of my brother. He's coming to pick me up, and I'll join him at his ranch. I have a tear in my dress, and I forgot to carry a needle and thread. Have you any?" She spoke with a slight accent with a southern twang to it, but Amy couldn't work out where she had come from.

"Yes, of course." Eliza stepped forward and, smiling, served the woman.

The woman scrutinised Amy from under her long lashes. That sideways glance had an appraising aspect to it that put Amy on alert. It was almost as if she knew who

Amy was, but was seeing her now for the first time. Why, Amy didn't know, but she didn't trust this woman. Her attire and her attempt at looking sober were giving a false impression, Amy felt. Not her usual costume, Amy thought, and could visualise the woman in more exotic garb. Each of the garments the woman wore was of the highest quality fabric, and cut and tailored by an expert. Amy had grown up in a busy town. She knew enough of fine fabrics and elegant clothes, and this woman was wearing the best.

"Have you both lived here and owned this store for a long time?" The woman asked Eliza, but again her eyes slid enquiringly towards Amy.

"Yes, I have lived here for some time, but Amy is new here," answered Eliza.

The woman smiled at the reply and nodded at Amy, but there was a knowing glitter in her strange, almond-shaped eyes that unsettled the girl. Unconsciously, Amy felt for the security of her Peacemaker in its holster. She didn't like this woman; she almost feared her. But why? What possible harm could this woman do to her? Amy watched as the woman left the store, needle and thread placed within her bag. The woman had given a last look towards Amy. Eliza had retired to the back of the store after saying goodbye to the woman. As the woman opened the door, she turned back and hissed, "Goodbye, Amy. Such a pleasure to finally meet you!"

Amy stood and realised that Eliza had not told the woman her name. Yet she had called her Amy. Unconsciously, Amy's hand caressed her Peacemaker again. The feel of the gun felt reassuring to her. She had been correct; her instinct had been spot on. The woman knew about her, knew enough about her to call her by name. What did she want? Amy was convinced that the woman exuded evil and had come to Nowhere to carry out something that... Here Amy faltered in her thinking. Who was that woman? And why was she here? Amy knew she had an evil purpose in mind. What was it?

CHAPTER THIRTEEN

Amy was sorting out the window display again for Eliza. The assortment of goods that sat on the table in front of the window had the fruit, vegetables, and fresh provisions that the general store had available. After each customer left, they had to be brought back to order.

Manuel and Josh had returned from their last delivery. Amy watched them as they both walked over towards the saloon.

"Manuel does not drink much, Amy, but after a tough day with deliveries in the heat of the sun, he always goes across to the saloon for one glass of beer. He enjoys it far more now he has Josh to go with him," Eliza said as she handed the latest batch of eggs to Amy for the display. Amy took the eggs from Eliza, noticing as she did so that the older woman was looking a little drawn. Amy knew that Eliza was expecting a baby – it was one of the reasons why she had asked Amy to help her in the general store in the first place – and Amy wondered vaguely when the little one might make an appearance.

Amy began placing the eggs with great care, but on looking out of the window, she saw the woman who had been in earlier follow Josh and Manuel into the saloon. Amy was astonished. Women rarely went into the saloon, unless they were of a certain type and class. Then Amy recollected the woman had said she was waiting for her brother. Perhaps she was looking for him in there. As she turned away, Amy saw that there were quite a few horses hitched to the rail outside the saloon.

Josh and Manuel went up to the bar to get their beer. There were several men scattered about the tent room. The room was shady, the sun dipping down below the horizon, leaving the encroaching shadows deepest in the four corners of the tent. That's why Josh didn't notice Abe and his two friends closeted together in the corner. They saw him, however. Abe rose to his feet after pointing out Josh and muttering about him to his companions.

"Two beers, please. It's been a hot day, and we have driven quite a way on today's deliveries. It's been a long, hot day, so we'll each have a whiskey first. They'll be most welcome," Manuel said.

Seth placed the two glasses of whiskey on the bar table in front of them. As he did so, a woman came in and rushed up to the bar. "Have you seen my brother? Has he been in here? You can't miss him. He's got red hair and is very tall." As she spoke to Seth, her voice loud and insistent, she seemed to stumble next to Josh. Her arm brushed against him and, with an insignificant movement that was unseen by anybody present, her hand swept across the open glass next to Josh. The small vial in her hand disappeared quickly into a pocket, its contents already clouding the whiskey before dissolving. "Oh, well, if you haven't seen him... I'll go back to the hotel and look there for him." With a swish of her skirts, she gave Josh a penetrating look before leaving the tent behind her.

Most of the men in the tent watched her leave. A beautiful woman like that was an unusual visitor in Seth's saloon. As Josh turned round to pick up his glass of whiskey, he was pushed roughly forward. Caught off balance, Josh sprawled on the floor. He looked up to see Abe standing over him, gloating as he lay helpless beneath him.

"I'll be drinking that! You owe me that at least for this

broken nose!" Abe said. He had come up behind Josh and shoved him away from the bar and onto the floor. Laughing triumphantly at seeing Josh sprawl on the floor, Abe lifted Josh's drink and began swallowing the whiskey down in mighty, lip-smacking gulps. He hardly drew a breath as he emptied the entire glass, placing it back on the counter.

"That was... That was..." The big man stood immobile, staring wildly around before clutching his stomach. Abe's hands grasped at his throat. His eyes rolled up in his head, and he crashed to the floor. Seth, the saloon owner, had only recently laid timber planks in that part of the tent in front of the bar. The noise of Abe falling to the floor seemed to echo around the canvas walls. The big man lay still for a moment before convulsing wildly in front of the horrified spectators. Then he lay still. Not one person gathered around him failed to realise what that meant.

"He's dead." Seth's voice boomed out in the sudden silence. "What ails the man? Why did he fall dead like that?"

The new young man, Zach, who helped around the bar (collecting the empty glasses and fetching and carrying the drinks required by customers) stepped up to the counter. He lifted the now empty glass and sniffed it. "Poison, I reckon it's poison." Hurriedly, he put the glass back down on the counter. Zach grimaced. "Yes, that's poison."

"I never poured out a glass of poison," exclaimed Seth. He picked the glass up then, also sniffed it, and nodded his head. "Zach is correct. There's poison in this glass." He then went towards Manuel's glass of whiskey, took one sniff, and shook his head. "This one's fine, and I know myself the bottle was all right earlier."

This conversation, about the poisonous glass of whiskey, took everyone's attention. Some men came forward. They also wanted a sniff of the poisonous glass and discussed it fully and in depth. Abe was forgotten. They even stepped over his body to discuss this peculiar glass of whiskey.

Josh didn't forget Abe. He looked down at the man and felt a cold shiver run up his spine, despite the heat of the day. Josh knew, without a doubt, that, thanks to Abe, he was still standing at the bar. That poisonous glass of whiskey had been meant for him. The realisation that the man, Duke, wanted him dead and would employ any means to achieve that horrified him. Still staring at the man who had died because someone wanted him dead, he jumped when Manuel grabbed his arm and pulled him to one side.

"By your expression, you think that the poison in the whiskey was meant for you, don't you, Josh? This is the work of the man who wants you dead, isn't it?" Manuel whispered in his ear.

"I expected to be shot or ambushed, but I never thought of poison. How did it get in my glass, Manuel?" Josh asked his friend, his voice harsh as the reality of the situation sank into him.

"The woman did it. Isn't poison a woman's weapon?" The voice of young Zach interrupted their conversation. Both turned to look at him. He'd only been in the town a short while and had joined Seth to help him run the bar. A tall, thin young man, his light brown hair and brown eyes made him almost insignificant, and his quiet manner and soft voice kept him at the back of any crowd.

"Yes, you're right, Zach. It must have been that

woman that came in. She brushed against you, Josh. When we were at the bar, she must have dropped something in your glass," Manuel said, his voice full of horror that a woman should stoop so low and so brazenly in front of so many witnesses.

"You'll never prove it, no way of knowing who did it, but I reckon it was that woman," said Zach, clearing up some glasses. "Best keep a lookout, Josh, someone's got it in for you. Wonder what will happen to you next?" Zach eyed Josh with interest.

"I wonder!" said Josh, and walked out of the bar.

CHAPTER FOURTEEN

Swirling the whisky around on his tongue, Josh felt the warmth of it slip down his throat, smooth and with the depth of an unusual taste. Josh took another sip, again savouring the unusual taste. "This tastes good," he said with a sigh, relaxing in the chair.

"That's because it's of the finest quality. I think they put molasses in to give it extra flavour. My husband liked to drink excellent whiskey and smoke a fine cheroot. He sent away for these cheroots. When these are gone, that will be it. I don't know where he got them from, and I really must give up smoking them. But I will enjoy the few I have left. God rest his soul, he had excellent taste."

The silence between them was amicable, and Josh was surprised at the obvious satisfaction of the woman beside him as she sipped at the whiskey and smoked her cheroot. The moon, which had previously lit up the scene before them, went behind a cloud, and it was only the glow of the cheroot Josh could see in the almost complete darkness.

There had to be a reason, Josh reckoned, so he sat quietly and waited for the older woman to finally tell him what was on her mind. Her attitude did not seem to bode well for the news she was about to tell him. Was he being brought out onto the porch to hear bad news? Nancy had invited him to have a last drink with her before they went to sleep. It had been unusual coming from her, but she'd been most insistent.

"It's Luke. He's getting worse, Josh." The words were blunt and to the point, and they were what Josh had somehow expected. But they still came as a shock and extremely unwelcome news. He had hoped that Luke, who seemed so much livelier, was getting better. These, he now realised, had been false hopes.

"How do you know, Nancy? I thought he'd been looking better lately."

"He has been looking better. You're quite right, Josh. I thought to myself he looked as if he was fighting the disease and improving slowly," Nancy said, her voice breaking slightly.

Nancy does care for him, Josh thought. He knew she liked all of them, but he hadn't realised the depth of her feelings for Luke. "What has happened? How do you know he's getting worse?"

Nancy raised the glass of whiskey with its remnants swishing around, and she took a deep sniff of it, revelling in its unique smell. Lifting the glass to her lips, she drained the lot and placed the empty glass down on the floor beside her with a thump. The moon had now come out once more. The hills to the side of Broken Horseshoe Ranch reaching up to the mountains were bathed in moonlight, giving them a harsh, icy glare on their jagged rock faces.

As he looked at Nancy, Josh saw her face showed deep lines from the light of the moon, throwing every wrinkle into deep shadow. Those lines had grown deeper over the last few weeks.

"What can I do, Nancy?" Josh asked the older woman, knowing there was nothing much he could do, but hoping she could think of some little thing that might help in this tragic situation.

A deep breath followed another puff from her cheroot. "He's beginning to cough up blood now. You know what that means. Don't tell Amy, she will know soon enough. Ben must not understand how ill his father is, so don't tell him either."

"Oh no! What can I do, Nancy? How can I help? There must be something I can do," Josh asked the older woman yet again, knowing deep in his heart that there was nothing anyone could do to help the dying man.

"I know you're working at the general store two days a week, but if you can, please go out with Amy every other day to search for the gold. Finding that empty casket and the map has given him so much interest and renewed his faith in himself. He feels he made the right decision in coming here, and that his faith in the Jesuit map was not a false hope. If you and Amy could progress with this search, it would keep his mind alert and focused on something other than himself." The words tumbled out of Nancy, her voice low so that the others would not hear it.

Josh felt all the intensity behind those words of Nancy's and agreed with her. "I can see he became fired up with enthusiasm when we found the new map. Tomorrow we go into the general store, but can I suggest you get Ezra and Luke to plan a route for us to take the following day? Luke can copy the instructions out for us to follow, as Ezra is not up to writing. Would that help, Nancy?"

Her hand reached out and squeezed his hand with a tight grip. "Thank you, Josh, that will keep him occupied most of tomorrow." Nancy took a last puff of her cheroot and put it back in her pocket. At Josh's surprised stare, she laughed. "I don't smoke a lot. One of these can last me a full week. Appreciate the fact they're no good for me, but it just calms me down in the evening." Nancy stood up and patted Josh on the shoulder. "You're a kind man, Josh Barnes. It was a good day that Amy found you and brought you back with her to Broken Horseshoe Ranch."

Josh sat on for a while in the dark. Then he rose and crept into the cabin, placing the block of wood they used to lock the door in place behind the door. He slid between the quilts, taking care not to wake the sleeping boys. He was certain that he wouldn't sleep. There seemed to be so much going on in his mind. Yet, before he knew what had happened, Ben and Chan had woken up and were getting up to do chores.

"Why are you so tired, Josh? Come on, you'll be late," Ben said to Josh as he came out of the cabin door, yawning. Ben had brought the horse and buggy around and was waiting for them to appear from the cabin and set off for Nowhere.

Nancy followed them out and waved them off. She gave a significant nod to Josh, who in return nodded back. He had been given a task to complete. Nancy wanted him to find the Jesuit treasure. That was no straightforward task, but this family meant so much to him now. Josh was determined to do his best. Now, he was just as eager as Amy to seek and find the Jesuit gold.

CHAPTER FIFTEEN

Amy was sorting out the sacks of beans in the general store. It was their biggest seller, and they arrived in huge sacks. Not everyone wished to buy in such bulk, so it was Amy's job to weigh out smaller portions which could be sold easily to the customers. The paper bags containing the beans were stacked neatly along a shelf. When she had finished that task, Amy walked to the front of the store where she could hear Eliza chatting with someone. Amy didn't recognise the voice but was conscious of a northern accent, certainly not the usual accent in this locality.

"Amy, you must meet this gentleman, Mr Charles Roberts. He has just arrived in Nowhere and is staying at the hotel. He hopes to set up a business here." Amy walked forward to shake the outstretched hand of the tall, handsome man confronting her. His smart suit and polished black shoes were distinctly out of place, as were the gold rings on his fingers and the elaborate watch chain on his elegant waistcoat. He smiled at her, his glance sweeping up and down her body in a manner to which Amy took exception. His hand lingered too long in hers, and Amy pulled her hand back swiftly and wiped it surreptitiously behind her back.

"How charming. I never expected to find such a beautiful young lady in such a desolate place as this. You will certainly make my stay much more agreeable. I hope we can further our acquaintance more closely in the future."

His voice was so artificially flattering, and the smile he gave her verged on leering so that Amy felt inclined to punch him in the nose. But she smiled sweetly and murmured her thanks. A movement behind her had Amy turning around to see both Josh and Manuel standing behind the women and listening to this conversation. Josh had a dark look on his face and glowered at the man. He found it difficult to shake hands with him when he and Manuel were introduced by Eliza.

"I am in the process of buying the old Thompson property, and I propose to subdivide it into small portions of land for all those people who are eager to move out West and join you all in living in the town of Nowhere. So it's wonderful that I have met with another businessman in the town, and I will encourage all the newcomers to use your general store. In no time at all, you will have a bustling town full of customers!" Charles gave them a wide smile, showing all his white teeth, and turned to leave the store. "Delightful to meet you all, especially you, Miss Amy; I look forward to getting to know you better." He took off his hat, gave a flourishing wave with it, and left the store, but not before his eyes cast another admiring look at Amy.

"I don't like that man," said Josh. The grim look on his face as he watched Charles Roberts walk down Main Street darkened as he glanced at Amy, who was also watching the newcomer. But Amy's face had an inscrutable expression upon it. It gave nothing away to Josh about what she was thinking about the newcomer.

"That land he is talking about is poor, barren soil. Nothing will grow there, and it's no good for grazing. It's almost all rock, and there's no water there. The last people sank a well, but it eventually dried up. To parcel it off and sell it to unsuspecting buyers sounds like a fraudulent venture." Manuel spoke thoughtfully and walked to the door to watch as the man walked down to the hotel. "I think Charles Roberts sounds like one of those carpetbaggers: out to make money at the expense of everyone else."

"He had such pleasant manners, though, and he was so well dressed. I'm certain he means well," said Eliza.

Manuel and Josh exchanged glances without comment, with Manuel shaking his head at the folly of his wife. Amy suppressed a grin and took herself to the back of the store. She wasn't getting involved in this conversation. She had made up her mind instantly about Mr Roberts. Living in a busy town before moving to Nowhere meant that she was not naïve and had met conceited charmers like Charles Roberts before.

Josh and Amy had finished their work at the general store and were on their way home. As they drove along the rugged track leading to Broken Horseshoe Ranch, Josh spoke. "What did you think of that chap who came into the general store?"

Amy glanced over at Josh. His voice was different, and she realised he'd disliked the man. Why? What had he got against him? She wondered as she thought about the encounter in the general store. Could it be that Josh was jealous because the man had flattered her and suggested he wanted to see her again? Amy wasn't sure how she felt about that. Did she want Josh jealous of someone paying her attention? She admired Josh, but she made sure her feelings for him were hidden deep within her. Amy had to think of him as a brother. Nothing more was possible. When he recovered his memory, he could remember another life, and maybe that life included a girlfriend or even a wife. No, Josh had to remain a friend, possibly a brotherly type of friend. That was all. Amy felt that, for her emotional survival, it was the only way she could think of him. But she had to admit she had a happy feeling when she thought he was jealous of Charles Roberts.

Josh spoke again. "Is Manuel correct in saying that is poor land, and too arid for farming, with no water?"

"I have heard that it's not very good. It was for sale at the same time as Broken Horseshoe Ranch. Ezra told us on our arrival we had been fortunate in the choice we made. Our ranch is a much better proposition, especially with the year-round water. The previous people at that ranch dug a well, but the water in it didn't last for many years and now there is little chance of water except after the heavy rains and in the winter," Amy said.

"I think the entire plan sounds as Manuel says, possibly fraudulent. That guy is not trustworthy, and I just did not like him at all. You don't like him, do you?" Amy noted his voice was sharp with anxiety. Josh was really worried about her feelings for this man. It was very difficult, in so many ways, to understand Josh. His blonde hair, bright blue eyes, and clean-cut, rugged good looks made him appear open, friendly, and with a character easy to read. But in the time since she had met him, Amy realised this was far from the truth. Josh had lost his memory, but he also kept within himself the feelings and thoughts that he had experienced since his arrival at the ranch.

An impish thought took hold of her. "I thought he was very handsome, and he was so smartly dressed." Amy didn't say exactly what she thought of Charles; time enough to tell him what her actual feelings were for the land agent. Out of the corner of her eye, she saw his face darken with displeasure, and she suppressed the bubble of merriment that was within her.

They drew into the ranch after a strange silence between them. "I didn't like him at all, or how he was flattering me." Amy had relented, realising that she did not want to have any unpleasantness between them. But it had been an interesting feeling, knowing that Josh did not like anyone flattering her. Or was it just that man he disliked? Why did Amy enjoy the thought that Josh had been jealous of Charles?

CHAPTER SIXTEEN

The grey dawn heralded the sun's arrival. Golden light could be seen above peaks around the back of Devil's Mountain when they set off towards their new search area. Amy shivered and thrust her hands further into her leather gloves. She pulled the collar of her heavy jacket tighter around her neck. They intended to look over the area alongside the track shown by the map, to see where the likelihood of Jesuit clues would be possible. It had been agreed, when they were all sitting at the table with the maps spread out, that both Josh and Amy were now more experienced and should find it easier to spot the clues.

"You know exactly the sort of area where the Jesuits will place the clues to their hidden gold now. Do rely on your experienced eye. Both of you have an instinct now, honed with that last expedition. Use it and don't ignore it," Luke said as he rose to his feet before going to his bedroom. At the doorway, he turned back to them both. "But you must take care. No gold is worth either of you becoming injured or losing your lives. Remember that, and be vigilant in your search." The door closed behind Luke as he went to bed. The figure that had stood in the doorway and pronounced these words was a frail shell of the man that had arrived at Broken Horseshoe Ranch. It had only been a short while – only months, not years – that had seen the deterioration of the man. His figure, with the light from the oil lamp cast over him and the shadows behind him, had emphasised his deterioration. No one said anything, but somehow, with that realisation of Luke's failing health, it was a solemn group that finished the discussion and got ready for an early start in the morning.

They had discovered the Jesuit map they were now using in a box hidden in a cave beneath an overhanging rock face. "This must be authentic. That's if it's not another false trail set by the Jesuits to thwart treasure hunters. I've not forgotten that booby trap that nearly killed us when we found that cave. We must take extra care. Those Jesuits were devious!" Josh said, shaking his head at the difficulties and dangers they had already faced.

The trail that led away from the ranch was a well-used one, leading from Broken Horseshoe Ranch and Dry Creek Ranch over towards the back of Devil's Mountain and towards the Avon River. The pearly haze on the horizon showed the imminent arrival of the morning sun and gave them enough light to travel on this trail at an easy pace.

"I have only been along here once, and then we turned back. Ben and I explored it one day after we first arrived. We used to take these short rides out from the ranch in different directions to get to know the surrounding area. Ezra told me he and Bella travelled around this area exploring every bit of it. According to the map, we go alongside the creek bed of the canyon. I imagine it's quite a sight after a heavy rain, so I'm pleased that it's been dry this year," Amy said. "I've never been further along this way before. All the maps showed the trails to search for gold up around the foothills of the peak of Devil's Mountain. That's where the rock faces and canyons have jagged peaks, small canyons, and many overhangs and caves. This way we travel along a river, which most of the year round is still flowing, despite the hot weather," Amy said as she guided Bella around the narrow track which led upwards.

Josh, who was following her, found this scenery much more to his liking. There were trees, a few sycamores and even the occasional oak tree. The vegetation was green, with shrubs and small trees overhanging the river, and even the spiky cacti looked well-watered and happier. They were loaded up this time, and he was aware of his saddlebags being full. Being uncertain of how long the journey would take to arrive at the first clue, they had brought enough with them for if they needed to camp overnight.

"That was such a good idea of yours, Josh. Pa and Ezra spent so much time yesterday organising today's route, it occupied Pa and he looked much better afterwards," Amy said as they rode along. Amy's voice held a hopeful note, and Josh could only look at the girl with sympathy. He didn't reply, as there was little he could say. Josh gave a noncommittal grunt as his feeble answer.

Neither of them needed to look at a map. They had looked at the map again and again and knew it off by heart. After a while, they travelled silently on their way. There was no need to say anything. Each was intent upon their thoughts as the journey continued. But it was a companionable silence.

They stopped at a small clearing for lunch, beside the tiny river that gurgled along beside the track. "What a difference from that last journey in all the heat of the desert, and that narrow canyon where the sun bounced off the walls and practically fried us." Josh had drunk his fill, bending over the running water, cupping his hand and letting the water flow out as he drank. He laughed at Bella, who stood beside him and slurped the water. "Bella loves it here. What a difference, girl, from that nasty, hot canyon, isn't it?" The horse paused in her drinking and looked at him as if she was agreeing with him. Then she dipped her head down again into the water.

Amy had already drunk her fill and eaten the lunch Chan had put together for them. She was turning around and around with an intent look at their surroundings. They were going to find the next clue. Amy was determined. She had to find something to keep her father interested, and to keep him alive! "From what I remember of the map, this creek becomes narrower and the sides become steeper, and then we should find the large boulder with a hole in it further on."

About an hour later, as Amy had predicted, the canyon became narrower, but there was still no sign of the boulder. The going became harder, the path became pebbly and the ground uneven, and the horses had to pick their way with care. As they continued, there was no boulder with its hole in the middle.

"It's another trick! Those Jesuits are at it again. There's no clue. We're just wandering around following another deceitful map that those twisters have left for fools like us." Josh was getting angrier and more frustrated by the minute.

Ahead of him, Amy had turned a corner of the canyon. "Josh, come and see this! This is amazing. I've heard about them, but I never thought we'd see them. Josh, you must come and see this!"

CHAPTER SEVENTEEN

Josh stood gazing across the land in front of him. The sun was now up, and the far off rocks and hills glowed red. In the distance, they faded into a misty purple and then into a blue haze.

"Is that the country that the land agent is hoping to sell in small blocks back east?" Josh asked Amy, pointing to the parched, arid land that stretched out far away from them. It was such a contrast to the lush vegetation that grew near the river beside them. "Does anything grow there? Who has been living there? I see a small wooden building in the far off distance. Was that the homestead?" Josh had shaded his eyes, squinting as he tried to make out the tiny wooden speck in the distance.

"Yes, no one has lived there since we moved here. Ezra told us that a man came out trying to farm it but lost all his livestock after the well he dug ran dry. It was up for sale when we bought Broken Horseshoe Ranch. We were told that it was a thriving property, and Pa thought long and hard about buying it, but fancied being near to his Jesuit gold map," Amy said as she came to join Josh at the top of the ridge.

Josh just nodded. He'd heard this story before. Considering the impetuosity of Luke in relocating the family to the Devil's Mountain area, it was a wonder he hadn't bought the bad ranch. "If the previous rancher couldn't make a living, how are folk going to survive on even smaller plots of land with no water? That man is a crook. He shouldn't be allowed to sell those small plots of land, giving hope of a new life to poor people scraping a living and trying to get by." The vehemence in Josh's voice surprised Amy. But she could only agree with him.

"What's the next clue? Was it to look out for a large boulder with a hole in it, and then go on to a small waterfall in the canyon below?" Josh asked Amy. "Have I got that right?"

It had been Amy who had joined her father and Ezra looking over the map. She was used to this country area and knew how to read it. As a newcomer, Josh left the navigating to Amy, feeling that his inexpert opinion would not be appreciated.

"Yes, Josh, it's a small waterfall. We should see that next. When we reach the waterfall, then we should be able to see the boulder with the hole in it. It must be round the bend in the canyon. Hurry, Josh," Amy was eager as they were nearing the end of the guiding clues on the map.

Josh immediately guided his horse, Star, around a large boulder to follow Amy along the length of the canyon to where it turned a corner. Her excited voice intrigued him, and Josh wanted to know exactly what it was she had found.

"Look! Up there. Can you see them? They are cave dwellings. They have been there for hundreds of years. Even the Indians didn't build them. They say they were here before the Indians came. Aren't they fantastic? Imagine living up there. Almost at the top of the mountain, and able to see for miles around." Amy was sitting on Bella, her face upturned towards the high cliff face with the dwellings carved out looking down upon her. There were stone built walls and openings for doors and windows. There was no apparent pathway up to them. Josh could only see rocks and boulders leading up perilously. There would be no easy way to reach those dwellings.

"Josh, what do you think of them?" Amy was surprised. She hadn't heard anything from Josh. Surely, he was amazed and intrigued by the cave dwellings up high on the cliff face? "Josh, what do you think of them?" She turned round to look at him, to find that he had his back to her and the cave dwellings. "What is it, Josh? What are you..." Amy's voice faltered, and she found she couldn't speak anymore. No wonder Josh hadn't answered her. She realised now what had caught his attention.

"The boulder with the hole in it. Look, Amy, it's up there, halfway up the cliff face. It's unmistakable. It's the largest boulder around, and look, it has the most enormous hole in it. That's the one we're looking for. Amy, we found it!" Josh was elated, and the grin on his face told Amy of his excitement and delight.

"That's unbelievable. I wasn't sure we'd manage to find it. I even wondered if the map was a fraud, didn't you?" Amy asked Josh.

"Honestly, Amy, I've been doubtful that any of these maps were correct. I've even wondered if they were hoaxes. Surely you had your doubts?"

Josh's words were an earnest enquiry which touched upon Amy's thoughts. Amy dismounted and took Bella down to the creek before she answered. She watched Bella drink from the water. Her voice came hesitantly at first, and then Amy finally admitted to him and herself her real thoughts about the search for treasure. "I thought the map Pa had was a hoax, but he put such faith and trust in it. I didn't have the heart to tell him of my doubts. Then we followed the clues and found the box, and now we have another map. Josh, now I think the maps may well be real, but there may be nothing at the end of them.

They may be a hoax, or someone else might have beaten us to the actual treasure. I have to believe in the treasure, Josh, because I honestly think that's what's keeping Pa alive." Her voice broke, and she knuckled away a tear that slipped down her face. Those fears and doubts she'd always kept deeply hidden within her heart. Finding herself the elder sister and carer for an ailing father, Amy had struggled on, keeping those doubts deep inside her. It was difficult for her to admit to them.

Josh found little to say after this speech of Amy's. He agreed with her, and he too realised the importance of keeping Luke's hopes alive. "Right then, we're both in agreement. We go after this Jesuit treasure of lost gold wholeheartedly, with our doubts hidden from Luke. Who knows, Amy? We might find it!"

CHAPTER EIGHTEEN

They rested the horses whilst they wandered around beneath the boulder. There were no other clues jumping out at them, and they were realising this search was going to take some time. The afternoon was upon them, and a decision had to be made. Should they go home immediately? Or should they camp for the night and look again in the morning?

"We followed the creek bed to get here. But, Josh, if you look at the map, I'm certain we could find a route back to Broken Horseshoe Ranch, which would cut our journey by half. Do you agree with me?" Amy had spread the map out on a boulder, and Josh came over to join her. She traced with her finger the journey they had already made alongside the creek. Then, opening the scroll out even further, Amy showed how much quicker it would be if they cut straight across the desert land to the ranch.

"You're right, Amy, that would make it a much shorter journey. I suggest we return to the ranch now. We can set off earlier tomorrow morning to reach here, giving us a full day to search for the next clue. The boulder has been found, so it's just the last clue we have to look for," Josh said.

"I'm looking forward to telling Pa we found the boulder with a hole in it. Surely that will make him feel much better?" Amy murmured.

Josh gazed down at the map as he nodded. "Yes, it's a triangle. We could cut across, making short work of the journey. It's worth a try, Amy. I think we could get back to the ranch by evening. Yes, your father will be thrilled to find out that we found the boulder."

"How he would have loved to climb up and explore

those cave dwellings. I only wish we could bring him here to see them." Amy gave a sigh, looked up again at the cave dwellings, and then straightened her shoulders. "Let's have a last drink and be on our way."

After a few miles, Amy was regretting her idea of a shortcut. Not only had their path been difficult to find, but it had also been overgrown in places, and they'd been forced to get down from their horses to cut their way through the amount of heavy vegetation. But when they left the area fed by the creek waters, the vegetation became sparse, and they were into desert land again. Now, they had to contend with rocky ground and enormous boulders, which they had to go around slowly so that the horses took care of the difficult terrain. It had been late afternoon when they set off, but it was still extremely hot. The last rays of the sun seemed to lose none of their heat, and they were all grateful, including Bella and Star, for that last long drink.

The sun had set behind the mountains, the orange glow lighting up the sky behind. Still, they plodded on desperately, eager to see a familiar landmark, but with the increasing realisation that the surrounding ground was unfamiliar.

"What do we do now?" Josh paused Star. He looked around, knowing that he was completely lost and wondering if Amy knew the area.

"I don't know. All I know is that I had a mad idea, and I wish I hadn't thought of this so-called shortcut. Honestly, Josh, I'm lost. I'm going to do something which you may think is completely mad. I'm going to ask Bella to guide us home." Amy didn't dare look at Josh. What must he be thinking of her? How could she not know where they were? She had suggested this route home, but she couldn't find her way any longer. Could Bella? "Ezra and Bella have explored this area many times, he told me. I can only hope she remembers it and can take us back home."

"Bella, Bella," the horse pricked up her ears and her head moved to the side to hear Amy. "Bella, home. Take us home to the ranch. Bella, go home."

"Will she find the way home?" Josh asked Amy.

"I don't know," Amy replied. She patted the horse's neck and whispered into her ear. "Please, Bella, take us home."

CHAPTER NINETEEN

The ground was uneven, and the sudden shafts of moonlight between scudding clouds left them still unable to recognise their surroundings. Amy let Bella take the lead, conscious of Josh following behind with Star. "I'm still uncertain of where I am, but Bella seems to know where she's going," Amy called back to Josh, trotting behind her.

He grumbled. "I only hope she does know where she's going," reached Amy's ears, but she only smiled to herself. Bella seemed to move faster, almost as if she could smell her stable and the food that she knew would be waiting for her return.

The clouds drifted away, and the peaks of Devil's Mountain beside them grew more familiar to her. "Josh, I think I recognise where we are. Isn't that the large peak of Devil's Mountain to the right of us? Surely that's how it looks behind the ranch, don't you think so?"

Brought back from almost dozing, Josh, startled at Amy's question, looked around him carefully. "Yes, Amy, I think you're right." He urged Star forward to ride alongside Amy and followed her pointing finger. "Bella did it! Well done, girl! Look, Amy, there's the Broken Horseshoe Ranch sign. We made it, thanks to clever Bella."

Both horses now needed no urging and moved forward at a good pace, eager to get home. Amy sighed with relief. Her bright idea of the shortcut had not ended in disaster after all. "There are no lights on. They must have gone to bed. Expect they thought we were camping out for the night," she said.

They had passed beneath the sign and were

approaching the cabin, when a figure ran out from behind it.

"Look, Amy, who's that? There's someone there," Josh shouted, and jumped off his horse to run forward. "Who are you? What are you doing?" The figure, obviously startled at their arrival, dashed towards a horse standing beside the privy, a distance away from the cabin. Leaping onto the horse, the figure bolted across the vegetable garden and away into the darkness.

Amy had jumped off Bella and stood open-mouthed at the fleeing figure. Quickly, she climbed the porch steps as she heard the front door being opened. Her foot stumbled over some objects and, as the light flooded from the open door, Amy bent down to pick them up.

"It's a small metal rod, a feather, and some Bible verses on a paper scroll." Amy held them out for the others to see. After explaining the reason for their late arrival, Amy placed the objects on the table amongst the freshly brewed coffee in their mugs.

Luke stood with the scroll of paper that had the Bible verses written on it in his hand. Holding it in one hand, he smoothed it out with the other. "So many homes have been invaded by Shadowhawk, so many feathers and Bible verses have been left to show that he had been there. Unsettling, even frightening, these intrusions into people's homes have been, but no one's been hurt, and no one has sustained any dreadful damage to their property." Murmurs of agreement greeted these remarks. "What does concern me is, first, what is he looking for? And, second, what is he going to do to the person when he finds it?"

"Why do you think that's going to be a problem? There's been no damage, as you say. Surely he won't hurt anybody?" Nancy's voice held a note of concern as if she was just realising the possibilities of danger that could arise with Shadowhawk's burglaries after Luke's remarks.

"Luke, I think you've got the right of it. No one goes to all this trouble and leaves a calling card, which is more of a threat than anything else, without seeking some sort of revenge," Josh said, and he shook his head. "This has been going on for some time now. There must be some reason that Shadowhawk knows that the person he is seeking lives in Nowhere. Why doesn't he recognise him?"

"We'll go round in circles and still be none the wiser at the end of it. I think we'll have to wait until Shadowhawk finds the person he's looking for," Amy said. "But I don't think it's going to be pleasant for that person when Shadowhawk finally finds who he's looking for."

"These quotations mean vengeance is on its way for someone. What was done to merit such determination to find this person and exact vengeance on them?" Holding the paper, Luke read out the quotations.

O Lord, God of vengeance,
O God of vengeance, shine forth!   *Psalm 94: 1.*
The avenger of blood shall put the murderer to death when they meet. Numbers 35: 21.

"I think it means that blood will be shed. Someone in Nowhere must die." Luke intoned these words with great solemnity as he returned to his bedroom.

CHAPTER TWENTY

It was midmorning of the next day, and it was Chan who spotted it first. Motionless, he stared across the horizon and then pointed. "There's rain coming. Look, everybody, there are black clouds coming towards us."

Josh came to join him, a hammer still in his hand. Ben ran out of the new kitchen building, where he and Josh were putting up shelves. Not having to go to the general store and tired after last night's long journey home and the hassle with Shadowhawk, Josh and Amy were working around the ranch. Leah heard the cry from Chan and emerged from her cabin, where she had been preparing vegetables for the evening meal. Nancy and Amy had been organising bed linen for the new bedrooms. When Luke and Ezra joined the group, the entire complement of the ranch stood staring at the black clouds, which were rapidly approaching.

"That's not rain. It's grasshoppers! We're being attacked by a plague of grasshoppers. Quick, everybody, grab what you can and cover the crops!" Ezra's shouts betrayed his panic, and he began grasping at horse blankets from the stable and throwing them over the plants which were nearest to him. As they all still stood watching him in amazement, Ezra shouted at them. "Go! Get moving!"

Nancy yelled at Amy. "The sheets! Let's get them and all the towels." The pair rushed off and, taking the freshly washed linen, they threw it anyhow over the crops. Freshly watered plants stood straight and tall but were soon under a covering of haphazard linens and garments.

The cloud was getting closer every second. By now it could be seen that it was composed of millions of insects.

They stretched from horizon to horizon, covering the earth and blotting out the sun. "There is nothing else to put over the plants. There's still more of them unprotected. What should we do?" Luke gasped out as he stood, mesmerised by that ever-approaching horror. "There's so many of them! It stretches for miles."

The ridge behind the ranch had many small gullies and hollows that were hidden from sight of the ranch. From one of the smaller gullies, a figure ran toward them. He waved small branches and twiggy vegetation. "Put some of this over the rest. It may stop some of them from getting to the plants." In the frantic turmoil of the moment, no one asked who he was or what he was doing there.

"Good idea. Grab anything you can. Cover the seedlings first," shouted Ezra. Everyone followed his example and threw whatever they could find over the crops. They used straw from the stable, and Ben and Chan tore up the tender grass from beside the creek. The longer blades they plucked in handfuls, throwing them as best they could over the small seedlings they had only planted that very morning.

The droning noise grew louder, and the sky darkened. Swarming grasshoppers hid the light of the sun. The grasshoppers arrived. Grasshoppers seemed to erupt everywhere around them, almost as if they had emerged from the ground beneath their feet. Swirling in mad clouds, they got everywhere and on everything. The flurry of insects about them was in their hair, some crawling on their legs and arms, and flying into their faces, almost blinding them.

"Hit out at them!" Josh shouted. He took his shirt off and used it as a weapon, swatting grasshoppers onto the floor, where he stamped on them.

"They're in my mouth! And my eyes!" shouted Ben, who was using a piece of timber whirling round and round, hitting as many as he could.

"I'm killing lots of them, aren't you, Chan?" Ben looked at Chan. The small boy stood, staring open-mouthed at the figure who had emerged from the gully behind the ranch. Following his friend's gaze, Ben looked at the man. He was standing: his hands hanging loose at his sides and his head bowed. The black hair hung in a pigtail, and his clothes were an odd assortment. The typical Chinese shirt-like garment hung over a pair of woollen trousers. Well worn, they were frayed at the hems and hung over his bare feet.

"Thanks for your help with the grasshoppers. But who are you? And what are you doing here?" Josh said.

"Inside now! Everyone get inside. Come on into the cabin. We've got to take cover. There's nothing more we can do." Nancy spat out a few grasshoppers as she ran up the steps to the door. She waved her arms fruitlessly, trying to clear a path through the cloud that swarmed around them.

The others needed no second bidding. Josh was the last. He threw a rock down onto the tablecloth corner to anchor it, hopefully saving the seedlings beneath it. As he straightened up, he saw the figure of the man who had run up to help, standing looking at Chan. In that split second, amidst the swarming, noisy mess of grasshoppers, Josh realised who the helpful thief had been.

"Inside, Chan! Get inside now." Josh urged the boy to move. He ran towards the cabin and pushed the man in front of him. "And you! Into the cabin with you."

Chan heard the last words Josh had yelled out. He ran and grabbed the figure by the arm. With both of them, Josh pushing and Chan pulling, the three of them tumbled through the cabin door. Ben slammed it behind them. He'd already closed the shutters and now, with the door firmly shut against the invasion outside, they all stood panting.

CHAPTER TWENTY-ONE

It took time before the last of the grasshoppers who had entered the cabin with them were killed. Meanwhile, Chan had his arms around the figure and was sobbing quietly. Head bowed, the figure stood stroking Chan's head, his arms clutching him tightly.

"Chan is your brother," Josh stated the fact. Everyone realised the truth of it and stared silently at the man and the boy standing in front of them.

"It was you! You milked the cow and took my eggs," Leah gasped.

"You did the work around the place to pay for your theft?" Luke said, as he sat sipping a coffee. "Why didn't you come to the door? Why didn't you tell us who you were?"

"I needed to see if Chan was happy here. I needed to see if you were good people," was the quiet reply.

"What happened to you both? Chan never told us anything about how he got to America or what happened to him once he arrived here. For such a chatterbox, Chan, you have kept many secrets," Josh said, looking at the young boy and then his older brother. Chan, they all surmised, was about eleven years old. Chan's brother, Josh thought as he looked at him, could be no more than fourteen years old. Like Chan when they had found him, he was pitifully thin and had several bruises on his face which were a fading yellow colour. The older boy still held Chan close to him, his calloused hand constantly stroking his younger brother's hair.

"Our parents died, and our uncle sold us to an American man. We came out here and were separated. Chan got sent off on the train. I was sent to a silver mine.

Lots of bad men worked at the mines. There were fights and killings. My owner got into a fight and was shot. When he died, I left. I remembered where Chan had been sent and worked my way to Nowhere. You are good people, I see that." He paused for breath, his arms still tightly clasping Chan.

Nancy stood with her hands on her hips, looking the boy up and down. "You're not in trouble with the law? There's no one chasing after you?"

The boy shook his head and looked up for the first time, directly at Nancy. "No, no, I was working for the one man who had paid for me to come to America. When he got shot, the bargain was finished. I left before I was forced to work for another man."

Nancy stared at the boy, at the earnest expression on his face, and took her hands off her hips and nodded at him. "Just as well we've added more rooms to this place. Thanks for all the work you've put in around the place and with the grasshoppers. Have you any belongings hidden over in the gully? If so, you'd better get them. Chan, I expect you'll be glad to have your brother staying with us." Nancy lifted a hand, signalling them to be quiet, then clapped both hands together. "It's gone quiet out there. Have they gone?"

There was a rush to the door. Ben, who was nearest, flung the door wide open. Everyone tumbled out of the porch and down the steps to look around. The constant turbulence of the air, which had been the grasshoppers swirling and rolling around them, had vanished as they moved on. There was silence. Each one of them turned to stare at the retreating black cloud as it moved on to cause havoc and devastation in some other place.

"Oh my! What a mess. So much has been eaten," Luke

whispered. His words sounded loud in the sudden appalled silence that had fallen since the last of the grasshoppers moved away.

"Are any of the plants saved? Did our makeshift efforts protect anything at all?" Ezra rushed to the nearest sheet that had been anchored down over some of the tenderest seedlings. Tossing the anchoring rocks aside, he lifted the sheet and gasped with delight. "These are fine. Have we saved any others?"

They all scurried about the garden, lifting the makeshift covers. The decimated patches and the many dead grasshoppers showed exactly where they'd been, but those frantic efforts when they had spotted the cloud coming towards them had not been in vain. Some plants and seedlings, hidden from the grasshoppers, had survived.

This violent grasshopper plague which had engulfed Broken Horseshoe Ranch had left the entire group exhausted, frightened, and now suffering from the aftermath. There was so much devastation. The grass had gone, the few trees scattered around the spring were bare of leaves. The spring itself contained the floating bodies of yet more grasshoppers. Surviving the grasshopper plague, they were stunned at the magnitude of the disaster that had befallen them.

Nancy, of course, was the first to recover. "Leah, go to the kitchen and set about cooking an early meal for us all. Boys, clear the debris from the spring and the channels leading up to the garden. Amy and I will collect all the tablecloths, sheets, shirts, and everything else we used. It will all need washing! The rest of you, clear up what you can."

It was a weary crowd that sat down for a meal that

evening. The boys (including Chan's brother, Tom) sat on the porch steps. Leah, Ezra, and Luke sat beside Nancy at the table. Josh and Amy, on the porch bench, leaned back against the cabin wall. A silence from exhaustion engulfed them all.

"Thank you for everything you did today," Luke said, and rose to his feet. The plate before him was pushed away, and he fell forward. Only Nancy and Ezra's strong arms as they jumped to their feet to grab him saved him from a heavy fall.

Amy dashed in from the porch, eager to reach her father. "Pa! What's happened to him? What's wrong with him?"

CHAPTER TWENTY-TWO

The excitement and drama of the grasshopper plague had worn Luke out. The next morning, there was still much to be done clearing up after the devastation the insects had wrought upon the property. Exhaustion had meant they all went to sleep without realising how bad things were.

"It's worse than I thought. The ranch looks terrible this morning."

Ben's voice woke Amy and Nancy, and they stumbled out from the cupboard they called a bedroom to join Ben on the porch. Tom and Chan were already there, having followed Ben out. Josh, an early riser, had been sitting on the porch for some time.

"Everything. They took everything green. What will we do? How will..." Ben's voice broke the horrified silence that had left everyone speechless in the aftermath of the grasshopper plague.

"We do what we have to do. We carry on as best we can. " Nancy stood at the porch railing, a man's dressing gown belted tightly around her ample figure. The long, grey hair, usually worn in a bun, hung in a braid behind her. Josh, seated on the bench, realised how frightened and upset the woman was. Normally, Nancy seemed to be bulletproof. That was the only way Josh could think of her ability to override any storm and work her way out of any unpleasant situation. But was it only the grasshopper plague? No. Josh screwed up his eyes as he stared intently at the older woman. It wasn't only the grasshoppers, was it? It was at that moment both Amy and Josh realised Luke hadn't joined them. Amy, who'd been standing beside Ben, made as if to go into the cabin, but Nancy's arm stopped her.

"I heard your father coughing in the night. The exertion of yesterday took it out of him, Amy. After I got him a drink, he went off to sleep. I think you should let him sleep." The older woman put a gentle hand on the girl's shoulder. "I promise you, Amy, I'll look after him when you're at the general store. I think we need both you and Josh to work there to get supplies in for us. We have little enough left from this terrible disaster."

"Look! Someone's coming." The keen-eyed Ben had spotted the rider before anyone else. As the man got closer, it was Nancy who recognised him. "That's Bill. What's he doing here?"

The group stayed on the porch. An early morning arrival was something unusual and could not be missed. The horse drew up in front of the porch, and Bill flung himself off and rushed up the porch steps, waving a sheet of paper.

"He came! Shadowhawk came last night. We don't know how he got in. This morning we found all the documents over the floor, a feather, and a Bible verse." Bill handed Nancy the verse.

Nancy glanced at it before passing it on to Josh. "What's happened at Dry Creek Ranch? How bad is it there? Did you have the plague of grasshoppers as well?" she demanded of the man standing in front of her.

"As bad as here. Looking at your patches of green, you acted like we did. We saved most of the vegetable plot. Ours is much smaller than yours. We covered it as best we could. Been told to ask if I could work here now. Not much for me to do at Dry Creek. Miguel says can I stay here?"

Nancy, looking at the paper again, was thinking hard. "Remind me, Bill. Before the war you were a teacher, is that right?"

Bill shuffled his feet. He pulled up the worn brown trousers he wore, straightening the gun holster that hung over his hip, and tucked his jacket closer around him, despite the increasing warmth of the sun. "Yes, ma'am, before the war I taught. But I'm learning how to work on a ranch, even with my handicap." It was apparent to Josh that Bill was fearful of being turned away from the ranch. With his disability, work was difficult to find, and Josh suspected that his allegiance during wartime would not be popular in this area.

"I don't need you for ranch work, Bill. I need you to teach." Nancy's words surprised everyone, and there was a general movement to listen closely to what was coming next from the woman. "I want you to teach Ben and Chan. Also, I'm not sure about Tom, he may need some additional teaching to bring him up to a good level of education."

"I have learning? The man teaches me as well as Ben. And my brother?" Chan's face was radiant with hope and excitement. He bounced on his feet, and the excitement burst within him and he rushed towards Nancy, flinging his arms about her. "Thank you, Mrs Nancy, thank you, thank you from the bottom of my heart."

Josh burst out laughing. "Ben is not so enthusiastic as you are, Chan. I think Ben would rather work on the ranch."

Nancy looked at her stepson and grimaced. "Oh well, two out of three isn't bad. At least Bill and Chan are happy. Ben, your father will be delighted that you are continuing some form of education. Surely you can be happy about that?"

Everyone looked at Ben. How was he going to take

this enforced education?

CHAPTER TWENTY-THREE

"Words can't describe this devastation." Amy and Josh were riding to Nowhere later that morning. The area between Broken Horseshoe Ranch and the small collection of buildings, cheerfully called by some a township, was mainly desert and supported very little vegetation. But, even here, there was a lack of anything green.

"No, you're correct, Amy. It's all too terrible," Josh answered after a few moments. He, too, was stunned by the surrounding land that had now been laid waste to. It was a solemn journey. Neither spoke again until they reached the scattered collection of buildings comprising the Main Street of Nowhere. "Manuel seems to be looking for us. We're not late, are we?" Josh called out to their employer.

"No, you're not late. I got up early. I couldn't sleep after the grasshoppers came yesterday afternoon. Josh, I want to get an early start. Goodness knows what state the ranchers will be in. They may have no produce for me, and then I'll have to decide how much credit I give them. It's not only those with crops that have been destroyed that suffer. This disaster will have a knock-on effect and will affect all the businesses in Nowhere. I've loaded up already, so let's be off." Manuel jumped up onto the waggon.

Josh scrambled up beside him and gave a farewell wave to Amy. Eliza came out to help Amy stable Bella, and when finished, the two of them walked into the store.

"Wasn't it dreadful? The sky went black with them. We had to shut all the windows because they were trying to get in to our vegetables inside the shop! What happened to you at Broken Horseshoe Ranch? And Nancy's ranch, Dry Creek. What happened there?" The words tumbled from Eliza's lips. Distressed by the events for her family and the other farmers and homesteaders, Amy now realised that this affected the shopkeepers as much as those growing their produce and trying to feed their stock.

She joined the older woman, who had been dusting various shelves with the tins and packets which were little used. Customers required only small amounts of some products, but Eliza made certain everything was kept freshly dusted, however little used it was. Amy took another duster and joined her, explaining in further detail how both properties had fared during the plague. The shop door opening gave its usual squeaky noise, and both women turned to see who had entered. Amy stiffened, her eyes widened, and she set her jaw unknowingly tighter, whilst her hand moved automatically to the Peacemaker in her skirt pocket. Amy's clothes around the ranch were practical canvas. Her skirts were shorter than normal, and she had sewn into the hems pieces of shot to weigh them down. The winds could be fierce and unpredictable, and an ordinary skirt could be whipped around by the wind. Having no need of such a skirt when tending the shop, she had resorted to a normal length of skirt, but had sewn into each one a couple of pockets. They were hidden by the seam. One held her trusty pocketknife, the other her Peacemaker.

"Good morning, ladies. Such a mess on the boardwalk and the street. Those nasty insects got everywhere, didn't they?" Carlotta pushed open the door and stood for a moment surveying both of them. Her eyes rested upon Amy, and a small smile flickered over her face.

Amy realised Carlotta knew they had guessed she was the one who had put poison in Josh's glass. Helpless, with no proof, Amy could only stand and stare at the sheer effrontery of the woman. Amy watched the woman as she walked across the wooden flooring to the counter. This morning, Carlotta wore another outfit. Again, it was of the most expensive material, a midnight-blue woollen cloth embellished with ornate braid and her collar had exquisite midnight-blue beads decorating it. Some years ago, on a visit to the dressmaker with her mother, Amy had watched, open-mouthed at the skill of, a woman beading a piece of cloth. A special candle holder reflected the light, and the poor woman was huddled beside it, straining her eyes. An outfit such as Carlotta was wearing cost a huge amount of money and was completely unsuitable for a place like Nowhere.

Eliza welcomed the woman, eager to serve this glamorous customer. Amy drew closer. She wanted to hear what the woman said. This woman, both she and Josh were convinced, had been sent to kill him. Carlotta knew who Josh was, knew his history. If only she would tell them something, some little clue about his past. Most of all, Josh, Amy knew, was desperate to find out who was seeking his death and the reason why.

"Has there been any mail for me? My brother still hasn't arrived, and I wonder if he sent me a message? Carlotta is my name." Carlotta asked Eliza as she stood at the counter, her elegant reticule resting on it.

Amy wondered if that little bag had contained the poison that had been intended to kill Josh. For such a small bag, it was packed tight with interesting bulges, and as she looked closer, Amy thought she saw the outline of a small pistol.

"The post arrives weekly. That's when the Stagecoach comes through. You came on it last Friday, didn't you? We only get it once a week, but not always with the post. It all depends on when it reaches Duloe. If there's not much in the way of letters or parcels, they wait until there's enough to fill a bag," Eliza explained to the woman.

"Oh dear, if my brother doesn't arrive today, I'll come in tomorrow to see if there's any message from him." She picked up her bag and looked around the store as if seeking to buy something. Then she looked at Amy pointedly before leaving the general store. "Take care of yourself, my dear, and your handsome friend."

"What did she mean by that? What an odd thing to say to you, Amy. Did you understand what she meant by it?" Eliza asked the girl with a furrowed brow as she watched Carlotta amble down the street towards the hotel.

"Oh, yes. I know exactly what she meant by that!" Amy also watched the woman, but she was not puzzled. No, Amy was furious. The woman taunted her and threatened her and Josh in front of Eliza. But it had not frightened Amy. It had been a warning, and Amy would heed that warning and be on the alert for whatever else that woman was planning. Amy was not afraid of Carlotta, she was furious with her!

CHAPTER TWENTY-FOUR

The day passed quickly. People came and went in the general store. Some women were in tears, and the men grim-faced as they faced hardship and possible ruin of all their hopes and dreams. Some had saved a fair amount of their crop, others had lost everything. The astonishing thing was that not everyone had been visited by the plague of insects.

"Mrs Granger's flowers were untouched. The grasshoppers didn't go near the Avon River valley. They came along in a great swathe across the foothills of the Devil's Mountain. It's amazing to go through so many ravaged plots of land and then come across green fields and healthy growing crops." Josh had entered the back door of the store and had been explaining to the two women the sights he'd seen on their trip with the deliveries.

Manuel joined him, shaking his head as he listened to Josh's words. "Incredible how one farmer has lost everything, but his neighbour's crops and land are untouched. Thankfully, so many are helping each other out. What about you, Eliza? What's happened in the store today?"

Amy longed to tell Josh about the visit from Carlotta and her warning. But that was for his ears alone. She'd wait till they had a chance to talk it through. The anger she felt for the other woman was overpowering, and Amy was surprised at the depth of it. Never had she felt this need for vengeance on a woman who was carrying out the orders of some unknown evil man.

"So many sad cases, Manuel. I've given some people essential supplies and put them into the credit book. So many have lost the crops they spent so long readying the soil for, I think they have lost heart. I can see some ranchers giving up and moving back to where they came from," Eliza said, tears filling her eyes at the predicament that so many of her neighbours and friends had found themselves in after the grasshoppers' visit.

Charles Roberts had entered the store while they were talking. He had been looking through some goods and collecting them to buy, whilst he listened to their conversation. A wide smile appeared upon his face, his white teeth flashed almost as much as the gold jewellery he wore upon his person.

"Eliza, dear lady, please give me the names of those who are likely to sell their properties. It's an ideal opportunity for me to buy them, split them up, and sell them on to others wishing to move out here – to a smaller, easier, more manageable plot." His eyes glistened with greed, and he moved forward to the counter, pulling out a notebook and pen, ready to take down the names. Unaware of the indrawn breaths of the others in the store and their horrified expressions at his unscrupulous ideas, he waved the notebook encouragingly at them. For a moment he couldn't understand why no one said anything, then realisation at how taken aback they were at his blatant attempt to increase his wealth at the expense of others dawned, and he tried to justify his position. "I'll be doing them all a favour, you know. They'll find it hard to sell their properties after they've lost everything. My prompt payment will enable them to move away, perhaps back home or into another new life. You see that I'm helping them out." The words fell into a silence. The silence said loudly that not one of them believed he was acting from the best of motives.

"I'm sorry, Mr Roberts, we don't have that information to give you. We know of no one planning to move away. It's all just idle talk after this latest setback of the grasshopper plague. Can I help you? Is there something you wish to buy?" Manuel guided him to where he had been looking and sold him the items he had gathered together. But no one gave him any names or showed any wish to converse further with the man.

"Goodbye, ladies. Looking lovely as always. Goodbye, gentlemen." Again he gave them the beaming smile, flourished his hat in an extravagant wave, and was gone.

"I told you, that man is a greedy shark! The sooner he moves away from Nowhere the better," Manuel said, a grim expression on his face as he placed the money he'd received from Charles Roberts in the cash box.

Later, after the work was finished for the day, Amy had sent Eliza to sit down and rest. The older woman was becoming larger the further along in her pregnancy she went. The work she did, she coped with admirably, but she had been upset and worried about those who had suffered with the grasshoppers. That added stress had tired her out. Amy also realised that she missed her son, who had been sent to help his grandparents after Manuel's mother had broken her ankle.

"I'm ready to leave now. Are you finished?" Amy called Josh, who was getting deliveries ready for the following morning. Manuel had been working from their list of orders, whilst Josh got the items ready for the waggon.

"I saddled Bella up to the buggy when I was out there last at the stable. Go ahead, Amy, I won't be long," Josh called out to her.

"See you at the buggy, Josh. Goodbye," Amy called to the others. She stepped out of the back door of the general store and went down the steps towards the buggy and the patient Bella. On the last step, Amy noticed movement beside Bella. Amy's boots were well worn, and the soles made little sound as she drew nearer to the noise across the yard. Amy thought she heard fabric swish and rustle as someone moved. She crept closer to the noise. Who was it? What were they doing?

CHAPTER TWENTY-FIVE

Amy saw the figure of Carlotta bending over the buggy. Puzzled, Amy, for a moment, could only stand and stare. What was the elegantly dressed Carlotta doing? Amy saw Carlotta standing beside the buggy with a knife in her hand.

"What are you doing?" Amy's voice rang out across the yard.

The woman jumped back from the buggy. She looked up and saw Amy rushing towards her. The tension left her face, and she tossed her head back and laughed at the girl. "What do you think, country girl? I thought it would be fun for you and Josh Barnes to take a tumble. This time he might die, and I'd love to hear that you would be hurt. Why did you have to come out and find me?"

Amy had reached the woman. She stared down in horror at the half-cut leather. "Why? Why do you want to kill Josh? What has he ever done to you?" Amy asked the woman. Her voice was harsh as she demanded answers from the elegant woman facing her; her expression sneering as she laughed at Amy.

Carlotta didn't answer Amy. She took a step forward, grabbed Amy's braid, and swung the girl around with all her might. The sudden powerful jerk threw Amy towards the side of the buggy, smashing her head into the wood. Amy sank to the ground. The blow had made her dizzy, and she was conscious of great pain in her face. Caught unawares by this sudden action of Carlotta, Amy raised a shaky hand to her head. She felt the blood trickling from her nose and mouth after her face had hit the wood with all Carlotta's force behind it.

Carlotta bent over her and hissed into her face. "Josh

has done nothing to me, nor have you. But I get paid for killing him, and you, I think, I will kill for pleasure." Again, she pulled Amy's braid. "I think one more time should see you unconscious, my dear, and then I can kill Josh without your interference." The voice purred its malice into Amy's ear, but she was no longer so dazed and was gathering her strength and wits. Amy knew she had to act fast or she would truly be as Carlotta desired – an unconscious body at her feet.

"I don't think so." Amy's voice was shaky, but her intention was clear. With one hand she grabbed hold of the wheel of the buggy to steady herself, with the other she grabbed her braid above Carlotta's hand, yanking it back from the other woman. She drew back her foot, shod in the men's boots that she always wore, and kicked Carlotta as hard as she could.

Carlotta screamed, and her hand fell away from Amy's braid. She bent down to rub her injured leg. "You bitch, I was going to leave you unconscious. Not now. I'm going to kill you, and I'll make you suffer for that kick! Several painful cuts should do it." The large knife she used to hack at the leather was held up high. It gleamed, shiny and evil, in the fading light of the sun as she prepared to rush Amy.

Amy scrambled back into the dirt, eager to get away from this madwoman and her knife. Her head was still dizzy, and she felt disorientated. She tried to reach for the gun in her skirt, but Carlotta was approaching her so quickly, she had no time to get it out of its pocket, aim, and fire. All Amy could do was edge backwards, hoping Carlotta would keep talking and give her that time. But the woman was laughing, enjoying Amy's frantic efforts to elude her and her knife. "This is fun! Aren't you enjoying this game, little country girl? What will your last words be, I wonder?" Again she gave that sneering laugh, waved the knife wildly, and made a move towards Amy.

The gunshot came from the top step at the back door of the general store. Eliza stood there with a rifle in her hand. Carlotta fell to the floor, her eyes rolled up in her head, and she lay motionless beside the buggy. Eliza had killed her.

Amy slid to the ground, leaning back against the solid feel of the buggy wheel. Her heart was pounding, and she was conscious of blood trickling down her face. Slumped in the dirt, in front of Amy, was Carlotta. The lustrous black hair lay spread out beneath her, the tightly wound bun having come loose in their fight. The midnight-blue woollen fabric of Carlotta's dress was darkening with the blood that was flowing from the wound in her breast.

"Is she dead? Have I killed her?" Eliza stood at the top of the steps, the back door of the general store behind her, a rifle in her hand. "You'd better check she's dead, in case she attacks you again with that knife." Eliza walked down the steps, the rifle still in her hands. Her face was set in hard lines, so different from her usual pleasant features. "Amy! Move yourself, girl, and check her pulse!"

The command from Eliza shook Amy out of her stupor. She knew she couldn't stand up because she felt so weak and dizzy. On all fours, she crawled towards the fallen woman. The out-flung hand nearest to her had held the knife. Amy held out a trembling hand and took hold of it. It was of the finest silver, made by a master craftsman. Polished to a fine point, she realised she had to take great care holding it because of that vicious sharpness. Another careful movement and she was finally at the body of Carlotta. Amy stretched out her quivering hand towards the woman's neck and felt carefully for a pulse. "She's dead."

CHAPTER TWENTY-SIX

Kneeling by the body, Amy looked up as Eliza came to stand beside her. Eliza still took no chances. She had not yet laid the rifle down. She held it still, ready for action. Both women stared down silently at the woman, who lay on the ground in the dirt.

"We don't know her full name, do we? We know nothing about this woman," Amy muttered. Shocked still, Amy was shaking. The sharp knife in her hand, which had been meant to kill her, was held so tightly that her knuckles whitened.

"There's only one thing we needed to know: Carlotta was a killer. We thought she was the one that put the poison in Josh's drink, didn't we? Now you find her tampering with the buggy. She was sent to kill Josh, but she would have killed you as well. Amy, can you stand up? That was quite a blow she gave you. Do you feel all right? I wish my son was here. It's at times like this you need a messenger." Eliza reached out a hand and helped Amy to her feet. A gentle hand pushed Amy's braids away from her face. "It's stopped bleeding, Amy, but you're going to have a bruise right down that face of yours. Can you go for the sheriff? Or at least into the store, where you'll find Manuel and Josh? I'll stay here with her body."

"The store. Yes, I'll go to the store. I'll be all right in a minute, it's just..." Amy rose to her feet, hanging on to the buggy for support. The solid wood beneath her fingers gave her a reality which she'd been finding hard to find. Everything had happened so fast; it was a blur in her mind, and she found herself reliving it again and again. "She was there, and she attacked me. I didn't expect it..."

"Amy, she was about to kill you! Look at that knife in your hand. Look at your skirt where she attacked you. I saw it all. You didn't stand a chance against her. She was a real fighter and was determined that you should die." Eliza grabbed hold of Amy's arm and shook it gently. "Amy, she's dead and you're alive."

Before Amy could answer, voices could be heard entering the stable yard. Josh and Manuel had come down the steps of the general store, and both stood still in shock as they took in the scene before them.

"What's happened? Are you both all right? Is she dead?" Manuel questioned his wife as he ran forward to stand beside her. He pulled her close in towards him. Finally, Eliza let the rifle go, and she thrust it into her husband's hands.

"Amy, you're hurt, your face is bleeding. Is that Carlotta? She's dead, isn't she? What happened here? Oh, Amy!" Josh ran forward and took Amy into his arms. His muscular arms around Amy made everything seem better, and she clung to him.

"I found her. She had a knife and was tampering with the buggy. She wanted to kill us both, Josh. Then when I found her..." Amy gave a great sob and buried her head into Josh's flannel shirt.

His arms tightened around her. "Oh, Amy, I couldn't bear it if anything happened to you," Josh said. Then a whisper reached her ears, torn unwillingly from him. "Amy, my life wouldn't be worth living without you."

Eliza told the story of Carlotta's attack on Amy. Both men praised Eliza for her skill with the rifle. "Grew up in a tough town; learnt those skills as a baby," the plump Mexican woman said with a grin.

Josh looked at her and the way she was handling the rifle and couldn't help wondering what other skills Eliza had learnt growing up in that tough town.

"I'm going to see to Amy's wounds. Manuel, sort out the damaged harness on the buggy. Josh, you go down to the sheriff's office. He will need to come back here and see to all this." Eliza waved a hand at the woman lying beside the buggy with the bloodstained dress.

The bustle began. Questions were asked and answered. People came and went, and the body of Carlotta was taken to the back of the sheriff's office. The gaunt figure of the Preacher, part-time sheriff, loomed over Amy as she sat in the general store nursing hot coffee. She had refused the brandy that Manuel had swallowed down in one gulp. Despite having choked on his own portion, he had been quite surprised that Amy had refused it.

"The thing is, she was a woman." The sheriff pronounced these words and looked down at both women. "Yes, she was a woman." Because of their blank expressions, he gave a great sigh and explained. "She has a room at the hotel, and her things are there. I'd like you ladies to go through them and see if you can find out the next of kin and then pack up her belongings. Don't fancy it, me being a man and all."

"You want us to go through Carlotta's belongings? But would that be right? I killed the woman," said Eliza, taken aback at the sheriff's request.

CHAPTER TWENTY-SEVEN

"Are you up to it, Amy? You're not too dizzy?" Amy and Eliza were being escorted along Main Street towards the hotel by Josh. Manuel had been left to sort out, with the help of the blacksmith, the damage to the buggy. He had also been charged by Eliza to clear up the mess in the stable yard. Amy had been transfixed by the blood, which had lain in a huge puddle in the dirt, after the removal of Carlotta's body. But now, she had another task, which she was dreading, in front of her.

"This is her room." The hotel owner unlocked the door for them and opened it. Joe Parker was a thin, weaselly-looking man. A thin moustache looked as if it had slid across his face and stuck awkwardly. His clothes hung on him as if he had thrown them on haphazardly when he rose that morning. Amy had saved Chan from being thrown out on the street after Parker's bullying ways could not get the young boy to work any harder. She had heard from other residents of Nowhere since then that he was a cruel taskmaster and spent much of his time trying to shortchange his customers. "Spent most of her days in here. Don't know what she was doing here for all that time. Good-looking woman but gave no one the time of day." He handed the key to Josh. Parker was about to turn away, but couldn't resist sneering at Amy. "Get any work done for you out of that little Chinese boy? No use to anyone. I'll bet you're sorry you took him on. Hope you're beating him hard. It was the only way you could get work out of him."

At the shake of Josh's head, Amy didn't answer the man. He shrugged at her silence and walked away.

"What a cruel, heartless man," Amy said.

"Yes, it's common knowledge that he treats all his employees abominably. There's nothing anyone can do. They need the work to survive," Eliza said, not without sympathy for those poor employees, but Eliza could see things as they were and accept them with no fuss. "Let's get to it then."

Newly built, when they had climbed the stairs up to the bedrooms, they were overcome by the smell of new wood. The hotel had been thrown up in a matter of days; so many men had worked on the project they were nearly falling over each other. But the hotel had to be finished in record time, said Joe Parker, and it had been. Pushing open the door, Eliza paused, taken aback by the mess in the room. The smell in Carlotta's room was overpowering. The newly built wooden room smell fought with the overpowering aroma of cheap perfume. It clung to their nostrils as they entered the room. Both women were appalled at the mess Carlotta had lived in. Expensive garments were thrown over the chair and the bed and hung from the dresser mirror. Furnished with an odd assortment, a chair, a bed with a metal bedstead, and a dresser with a mirror (which had a huge crack across it). The room was made worse by the messy clothes and the trunk laid anyhow on the floor.

"I'll wait outside," Josh said, and hastily retreated from the room.

"You look for papers and documents, Amy. I'll sort out the clothes," Eliza said and, putting the trunk on the bed, she began folding clothes.

"Stop, Eliza, wait a moment. Let me look in the trunk." Amy began feeling around the lid, searching for hidden compartments behind the cloth lining. "Nothing in the lid." Her hands patted the bottom of the trunk and the sides, searching delicately for any bulge or lump that might mean that something was hidden. Eliza watched over this search. There was nothing in the trunk's base. "Here! There's something here." Amy could feel something at the back of the trunk.

Loud voices outside the room reached the ears of the two women. "You pay me money before I let you take any of her stuff. I thought you were just going to check her identity, that's what I thought the sheriff said. If she's dead, I should get everything she left behind. You've no right taking it, that sheriff shouldn't have told you to. Her stuff is all mine because she was staying here." The weasel-faced man could be seen shaking his fist at Josh through the half-open door. Dirty hair hung over his shirt collar, which was worn thin, the fabric fraying at the edges. Trousers hung on him and were held up by greasy suspenders, the original blue colour now a slimy navy. His voice rasped at Josh, who was standing his ground against the man's tirade but was at a loss as to the legality of the situation.

Not so Eliza. She walked over to the door, flinging it wide open. "That woman told me you charge the earth for a poorly furnished room, and she paid upfront. There is no reason you should inherit anything from her. I'm going to take everything back to the general store, and I shall inform the sheriff of that fact. Then you will get your room clear and ready for your next customer." Eliza waved the piece of paper in front of the man's nose, letting him see the name of Josh. "Look what's on her bed! It says Josh Barnes on this piece of paper. That means she knew him, and he should inherit if anybody should."

The man folded his arms and glared at her. But Eliza

was not to be shifted, and he recognised this. At that evidence of Josh's name in front of him, he stomped off down the hall, cursing under his breath. Grumbling about rude, interfering women, he descended the stairs, leaving them alone to carry on the search.

"My name? Where did you find that?" Josh was thunderstruck at this piece of information.

"Well done, Eliza, that was clever thinking," Amy said from the doorway with a smile on her face as she closed the door behind the hotel keeper.

"I found it on the bed, Josh. But it says, '*Kill Josh Barnes*'. I folded over the kill word. We must get all this stuff belonging to Carlotta back to the general store and go through it. If there's any information concerning your predicament, Josh, this will be the best chance you have of finding it out." Eliza reached up and patted Josh on the shoulder. "Don't worry so much. Come, remember you're not alone. You have friends that want to help you solve this puzzle."

While Eliza and Josh were talking and looking at the paper, Amy had returned to the trunk and that suspicious bulge she had found earlier. Her fingers felt loose stitches holding the fabric together. "Carlotta was no needlewoman. I wonder if the needle and thread she bought from the store was to sew this seam up." Amy's murmurs as she continually worked at the haphazard stitches reached the two standing talking. They both joined her as she finally worked the layer of fabric apart from the inner lining of the trunk.

"There are gold coins in here and pieces of paper," whispered Amy to the others.

"Leave them where they are; pack up everything. Come on, throw everything in the trunk and let's get out of here." Eliza's voice held an urgency which galvanised Josh and Amy into action.

In seconds, they had left the room behind them. Josh carried the trunk, and Amy and Eliza each had clothes draped over their arms. "Hurry, before that man decides to use force to get whatever we found. Many disreputable men are hanging around the hotel he could use. Best we get back to the general store," Eliza said as they dashed along Main Street, round the back, and into the general store.

Amy shuddered at the sight of the bloodstain beside the buggy. Then her eyes caught sight of another bloodstain on the buggy itself. She lifted a hand to her face and winced again as her fingers touched the wound she'd received when her face had been smashed into the wood. Her lips tightened at the memory of the fight, but she quickened her step into the general store.

The back of the store, the hall, the kitchen, and the entire living space of Manuel and Eliza (including the large central table) were now covered with Carlotta's belongings.

"What are you looking for?" Manuel asked his wife. "What are you trying to find?"

CHAPTER TWENTY-EIGHT

"Here, take this carpet bag and look for secret compartments or anything hidden between the lining and the bag, Amy. I'll look through her clothes, searching for hidden pockets. I found the note with *Kill Josh Barnes* on it. Surely she will have some other information?"

All the clothes were piled high on a couple of chairs. The trunk was now on the floor. Laid out on the table were the belongings of Carlotta, and they could see what she had brought with her to Nowhere. A small beaded purse held a few coins. Hidden in the trunk, alongside the two gold coins that Amy had found, were several pieces of paper, all from a miner's banking company, in receipt of gold. But there was nothing else to explain why she was there in Nowhere, where she had come from, or where she was going to go next. The only documentation they had found was that piece of paper that said *Kill Josh Barnes* in that familiar handwriting.

Josh sank onto a chair. "When will it ever end? Why am I to be shot down, poisoned, or killed in some other newfangled method the next killer will produce? Should I leave here? I'm bringing danger to you all. I should leave. I'll let you get on with your lives without the danger of someone else coming to find me. Amy was nearly killed today. Abe was poisoned. Who will be next?" His head went into his hands.

Amy stood aghast at this complete breakdown of Josh's. She couldn't bear to see him leave. How would she cope without him? He was a part of their family, part of the group that made up Broken Horseshoe Ranch. It wouldn't be the same without him. What could she say to him?

Amy didn't need to speak. She wasn't alone in struggling to find the words to help Josh. Manuel was also struck dumb. Not so Eliza. Diminutive in so many ways and always self-effacing beside her more talkative husband, she was, however, never one to mince her words when there was a need for plain speaking.

"Have you quite finished, Josh Barnes? Why are you feeling so sorry for yourself? You should thank your lucky stars that you've survived another attempt on your life. We've made you welcome in our home. We are all eager to help you solve this puzzle of a killer stalking you. But if you're not grateful to us and wish to move on to better people and live in a smarter place from Nowhere, just feel free to go! As for bringing us danger with your presence here, all our lives are in danger. Living in Nowhere is dangerous because it's a frontier collection of houses and businesses. If you don't like us or want our help, just leave now!"

Startled at these outspoken words from the normally quiet Eliza, Josh straightened up in his chair and stared at the woman. "I'm sorry, I didn't mean... I'm so sorry. I'm grateful... I don't want anyone hurt because of me. Amy nearly died today." Josh's voice broke, and he looked at Amy with a look of such warmth it surprised the girl. "Carlotta would have killed her if it hadn't been for you, Eliza."

"Josh, we understand your position. It does you credit that you want to leave us out of any danger. But you're here now; you're one of the family. And we stick by our family. So no more of it, please. Let's get on with this distasteful task of searching through this woman's belongings." Manuel hitched up his trousers, straightened his suspenders, and gave Josh a bracing thump on the back.

"You've been told, Josh Barnes," Amy said, grinning at his discomfiture. All the while she was hugging to herself that look of warmth towards her that had crossed Josh's face. She didn't know what to make of it. But Amy treasured it, putting it to the back of her mind to be thought of later. Now her attention had to be on Carlotta's belongings.

"What a mixture of expensive clothes and cheap ones. I think this lady has known poverty at times, but then has had money to spend on luxurious items," Eliza said, holding a pure silk blouse.

"This perfume is cheap and nasty, but these dresses are made of the finest material, and trimmed with expensive lace and embroidery," Amy said as she smoothed down the fabric of an elegant green costume. "What should we do with it all?"

"The fabric, as you say, it's good quality, Amy. I'm going to cut it up into sizable lengths, strip off the decoration, and, if you agree, we'll take some ourselves. The rest I will sell and keep the proceeds in a fund for those hardest hit in the grasshopper plague."

They sorted it out into piles. They went through everything, felt pockets and fabric seams, anything that could have a paper or an object hidden which would help in their search for the identity of Josh's would-be killer.

"Nothing. Apart from this paper with Josh's name on it, the coins, and the paper money, there is nothing. What woman going on a journey, staying somewhere new, would have nothing on her person showing her destination or where she's come from?" Manuel said, looking down at the objects on the table. "She's been told to be careful. This is not your average woman. Someone gave her instructions on how to conduct herself and what to take with her."

"But who was that person? Who was that someone?" Josh said. "Who is going to such lengths to pay people to kill me... and why?"

CHAPTER TWENTY-NINE

"What happened to your face?" was the first question that greeted Amy on her return to the ranch late that night. The story of Carlotta and her death had to be told again and again.

Leah smoothed some special salve of her own concoction over Amy's face. Everyone exclaimed over the happenings in the stable yard of the general store.

"The sheriff decided Eliza acted lawfully, and since no one knew where Carlotta came from, Eliza and Amy should keep her belongings. He said to share the money between us, and Eliza's going to sell some of her bags and shoes in the store. It will go to help those hit hardest in the grasshopper disaster," Josh said.

Amy relaxed back in the chair, thankful to be back at the ranch, and tried to forget the horror of seeing Carlotta's body bleeding out in the dirt behind the store.

"Amy, you told us the other day that Carlotta had wonderful clothes. What's happening to them?" asked Nancy, ever the practical one.

"Eliza's unpicking it all, and the fabric and braids can be used again. Somehow it doesn't seem right picking over this woman's clothes and belongings," Amy burst out. "I know she was evil but..."

"Probably they were ill-gotten gains anyway. Better you make use of them, rather than letting them go to waste," Nancy said.

"Here's another one to add to the collection, Luke." Josh pulled out of his pocket the slip of paper they had found in Carlotta's room. The paper said, '*Kill Josh Barnes*', in the same script as the other ones.

Luke got up from his chair and went over to the secret

cubbyhole in the wall. Opening it, he brought out the other papers, returned to the table, and spread them out side by side. One merely said, '*Josh Barnes Broken Horseshoe Ranch*'. The others all said, '*Kill Josh Barnes*'. "The writing is the same, the paper is the same," Luke said.

Josh jumped to his feet. The chair clattered onto the floor, and he stood for a moment breathing heavily, an angry flush on his face. He leant forward and swept the papers to one side off the table. The dishes clattered, and a knife fell from a dish onto the floor.

"When will it stop? I should move on. I'm bringing you all into danger. Look what nearly happened to Amy today. That's on me! I'm bringing these killers into this family. I should leave now and let you all live in safety." Josh shouted these words and stamped up and down. The others watched him with varying expressions ranging from sympathy to annoyance. Nancy was annoyed and felt like giving him a good talking-to, but she could see that Luke was about to speak.

"When you have finally finished with the dramatics, Josh, please take a seat again. We understand the increasing frustration you feel, this constant need for care, knowing that someone is out to kill you and sending different people to do the job for them. Whoever wants to kill you, Josh, is a coward. If he was a real man, he'd come himself. You've proved to me you belong here, and for the present time, we need you. I want you to remain. Danger is part and parcel of the way of life out here in the West. We face it daily, and, unfortunately, Amy was in the wrong place at the wrong time tonight. She wasn't the target of Carlotta, you were. But she survived and Carlotta didn't. Josh, pick up the papers and put them away for me. One day, you will throw them back at the man who wrote them. Of that, I'm certain. One day, you will meet the man who's persecuting you." Luke rose unsteadily to his feet after his speech and patted Josh sympathetically on the shoulder as he strode off into his bedroom. He closed the door behind him, but not before they could hear him starting to cough.

The next morning, before they set off for the general store, Amy and Josh had to inspect the work that had been done the day before on the ranch. Those seedlings and plants that had been saved were now flourishing again, and the other ground had been dug over, ready for new plants.

"Well done. It all looks good now. You've all worked hard," Amy said as she stood with a hand on Ben's shoulder. "How are you settling in here at Broken Horseshoe Ranch?" she asked the older Chinese boy who stood close beside Chan. The two brothers were inseparable, but Amy was pleased to see that they included Ben and had become a threesome. It could have been difficult if the two Chinese boys had chattered together and left Ben alone. "I hear you are teaching Ben Chinese. How are you all getting on with your work with Bill? He was a professor before the war, wasn't he?" Amy asked the three boys.

"And we teach Chinese to them," Chan said proudly.

"He's good. Bill knows lots of stuff. Not like some teachers I had. They knew nothing. He's helping me with my writing," Ben said, but at a look from Amy, he added quickly, "of course, we do lots of other stuff, like maths and geography."

Josh and Amy rode out under the sign on their way to Nowhere. Amy began chatting happily to Josh.

"Everything seems to be going well at the ranch. The bedrooms are nearly finished, and the kitchen should be ready by the end of the week. Chan and his brother are a great help. They love working in the garden, and Nancy told them they will get a percentage of the profits. They were so excited. I think it will be hard to stop them working and make them rest sometimes," Amy said, delighted that all was well at the ranch.

Josh agreed with the girl but felt certain that all was not well. He'd seen Nancy's face that morning and realised that Luke had taken a bad turn during the night. Neither Amy nor Ben realised Luke was failing fast, and despite his determination to carry on living, it looked to Josh as if Luke was losing the fight.

CHAPTER THIRTY

"I want to do a stocktake today. It may mean working later than usual. Do you mind, Josh?" Manuel asked Josh, as he placed the last of the delivery orders onto the waggon. It had become routine now for Josh, and he and Manuel worked well as a team. Josh enjoyed the visits to the families of the properties they visited. For some families, it was the only interaction with outside people from month to month, a weekly occasion that was to be savoured and enjoyed. Manuel, knowing this, greeted everyone with cheerful conversation and the latest gossip from Nowhere.

"There are a few boxes of produce today, so many are struggling to find enough to feed themselves, let alone give to me to sell," Manuel said, looking at the waggon, having little fresh produce to sell in the shop on their return trip.

"Amy, can you take over for me in the shop?" Eliza's voice reached Amy as she was washing the floors after sweeping out the dirt that had been tramped in from the street. Amy dropped the mop and ran to Eliza's side. There had been a note of panic in the older woman's voice, which alarmed the girl.

"What's wrong? Don't you feel well?" Amy dropped to her knees beside the woman, who sat in a chair, gripping the arms of it tightly. "Is it the baby? Is it coming?"

"I don't think it's the baby, Amy. A few moments ago, I felt dizzy. I was up early this morning and started on the stocktaking immediately. There were so many packets and boxes to be entered on the list and counted up. I think I've just done too much," Eliza said to the girl, trying to reassure Amy and herself at the same time.

"Do you want a drink of water? Or a cup of tea? Or coffee? Perhaps I should bring you a glass of brandy?" Amy was trying frantically to think of what she should do to help the pregnant woman. She was there to do her best to ease the load on this woman during her pregnancy. What could she do to help her now?

"It's strange, my dear, but I don't like coffee anymore. But I would love a cup of strong tea. If I rest in the back, could you look after the store and carry on the stocktaking by yourself?" Eliza said, looking at the worried girl kneeling beside her. "Thank you, my dear, for being here. It's been such a joy having you to work with. I don't think you know how much I have relied upon you since you've been working here with me."

Relief flooded through Amy. She could help Eliza. A cup of tea, looking after the store, and continuing with the stocktaking were simple tasks she could carry out. Thank goodness she didn't have to deliver the baby. At least not yet!

The morning continued as normal, and Amy dealt with the customers and proceeded with the stocktaking. Amy insisted Eliza should rest that afternoon. There were few customers, most of the women who came in only wanted to chat, pass the time of day, and moan about the difficulties of living in a frontier town. Moving to Broken Horseshoe Ranch and living there with little outside contact, Amy now understood the loneliness that these women faced. Hardship with the primitive conditions they lived and worked in was bearable, but loneliness was a different matter, and it took a strong woman to overcome it.

Late afternoon saw Eliza get up and join Amy in the

shop. "Amy, thank you so much, my dear. I feel so much better. You were right. I needed a rest. You have done so well, it will only take us a short time to get it finished now." They were continuing with the task when Josh and Manuel returned. Both men were covered in dust and were exhausted after an unexpectedly hot day. The heat had risen throughout the morning and afternoon, and their journey had taken them longer than usual.

"I think you both need a drink and a wash," Eliza said, looking them both up and down. With a mischievous glance at Amy, she continued speaking. "I wonder which you will have first?"

"Now, Eliza, don't tell me you're going to become a nagging wife. But yes, we need a drink and a wash. And you guessed correctly, we're going to the saloon first," Manuel said and, stooping, kissed his wife on the cheek. "You're looking better, my dear. You were very pale this morning. Now you look so much better."

"I feel much better, thanks to Amy. I've rested most of the day, while she took over the store. Such a difference it's made to me," was Eliza's reply.

The saloon wasn't crowded. Seth was behind the bar as usual and greeted both men with their favourite drink.

CHAPTER THIRTY-ONE

"Come and join me. Have you just finished your deliveries, Manuel?" The Preacher, Nowhere's acting sheriff, sat on a stool at the bar with a large glass of whiskey in front of him. He beckoned to Josh and Manuel to join him and told Seth to fill up another two glasses for them.

"Yes, it's been a tough day. So many have lost their crops and find it difficult to make ends meet," Manuel answered the Preacher, inclining his head in thanks for the whiskey and taking a large gulp of the first one. He put the glass down, smacking his lips with enjoyment.

Josh took a tentative sip of his whiskey. He'd learned through experience that the whiskey sold in the saloon varied from one brand to the next. It wasn't a good thing to ask where Seth got his whiskey from. Not all of it was of a reputable brand. Some, he reckoned, came from a still out of the back shed. "This is an excellent whiskey," Josh's voice held surprise, and the Preacher laughed at him.

"Nothing but the best whiskey for the Preacher," said Seth as he polished a glass and placed it back on the shelf. "If I don't serve him the good stuff, he won't pray for me anymore. That way he says I'm certain to go to hell!"

Josh joined in the laughter, enjoying the easy friendship that had grown up between these men. From different walks of life, with varying backgrounds, they had been thrown together in the peculiar township of Nowhere.

The swing doors of the saloon hurtled back as a man rushed in. "Preacher... I mean sheriff... come at once.

We've caught the Shadowhawk. We have him." The men jumped to their feet, and the sheriff ran out the swing doors with the tails of his long black coat flapping behind him and his black boots pounding a tattoo on the wooden floor.

"Where, man? Where did you find him? How do you know it's Shadowhawk?" The sheriff shouted out his questions as he followed the man, who ran along Main Street and gestured to the hotel.

"We found him in Mr Parker's office, going through his papers," the man gasped out his reply.

"Where's Parker? Is he there with Shadowhawk?" the sheriff asked as he ran up the steps, across the wooden boardwalk, and into the hotel. Josh and Manuel followed. This was interesting, and both of them wanted to see who this Shadowhawk person would prove to be.

One of the hotel staff stood by a door with a large stick in his hand. "In here! He's in there. You'll never guess who it is!"

The sheriff pushed him aside and flung open the door, his gun drawn at the ready. He needn't have bothered. Sitting, calm and relaxed, in Parker's chair in his office and smiling at the sheriff was Zach, the young bartender from the saloon.

Before anyone could speak, Zach waved some papers at the Sheriff. "I've got them! At last, I've found what I was looking for. These papers will prove that Parker is not only a crook but a murderer." A satisfied smile crept over his face as he looked down at the papers he held in his hand.

Josh saw a feather lying on the floor, alongside a paper with the usual written Bible verses. They were not needed here, not now. The man who had terrorised the neighbourhood with his threats of vengeance sat in a chair with a sweet smile on his face.

"What's going on here? What are you all doing in my office?" Josh was pushed roughly aside as a travel-stained Parker strode into the room. His brows drew together and a frightened frown crossed his face as he saw the papers the young lad held in his hand. Everyone could see what they were. The large headings on them could be seen from across the room. They were land deeds, and there were several of them.

Josh heard the sharp intake of breath from the man. Parker moved restlessly beside Josh. He looked from one person to the other, standing in his office. "What have you got there?" His voice was no longer bold and brave. It held a worried note that Josh noticed had crept into it. "What's everyone doing in my office? Why are you holding my private papers? Give them to me!"

CHAPTER THIRTY-TWO

"I've got proof of your..." Zach began speaking. Before he could finish, the gunshot rang out in the crowded room. The smell and the smoke drifted about them, as did the cry from Zach which followed that gunshot.

"No! No, you don't!" Josh attempted to knock the gun from Parker's hand before he could fire again. Manuel, beside him, reached for the man's hands, hoping to pull them behind him. But it was the sheriff who acted first. His gun appeared in one fast movement, and Parker fell to the floor with a bullet between his eyes.

Meanwhile, young Zach was lying on the floor, blood seeping from a wound in his shoulder, and laughing uproariously. Everyone in the room stared at Zach, wondering if he had gone mad. "He shoots me! I'm the Avenger, and I'm supposed to shoot him. This isn't how it was meant to go." He pulled himself upright and sat leaning back against Parker's desk. One hand held the papers, the other held the bullet wound in his shoulder that was seeping blood. "Sheriff, this man was a killer. Every single paper here is a land deal. The owners were forced to sell or he would kill a member of their family. In my case, he killed all my family; my mother shoved me into a cupboard or I would be dead. I watched him turn his gun from my father to my mother and my little sister. That's not all. He was still doing it! Find out where he was this last week. I'll bet he was doing it again." Zack's face clouded with sorrow and anger. He crawled forward and looked down at the body lying on the floor beside him. "Murderer!" Zach said the word and then spat on the body.

"But why? Why was he killing everyone to buy up

their land? What's in it for him?" The sheriff stood with his gun in his hand. He held it loosely, but everyone knew his gun would talk! Everyone had seen how fast the Preacher /sheriff could draw his gun.

"The railroad. Every property is on the line that the railroad will take. Parker had inside information on the route it would take. He stands to make a fortune when the railroad company comes to buy them all up." Zach stood up. "I'm no good as an Avenger. I'm the one that gets shot! But, Sheriff, here are the papers. They're all on the far side of Duloe. Check with the sheriff living there, and while you're about it, check your wanted posters. I think you'll find Mr Parker under a different name and for different crimes. If you don't mind, I'm going to bandage this wound before I faint from lack of blood." Zach thrust all the documents into the sheriff's hand and gave a long look at Parker's dead body before walking out of the room, down the hall, and out of the front door of the hotel. No one stopped him; no one said anything. They watched him go in silence.

"Sheriff, shall we help you check out those wanted posters? Be good to know who that villain was." Manuel stepped back as the sheriff supervised the removal of the body of Parker to the backroom behind the sheriff's office. Parker would lie beside Carlotta. They deserved each other.

"Zach could have the reward if there's anything on Parker. If anyone deserves it, I think it's Zach, after all he's been through," added Josh.

"What about his break-ins as Shadowhawk? You going to put him in gaol for those, Sheriff?" Seth asked. "I want to keep him on, working for me in the bar. Don't think he did any harm, and it flushed that Parker guy out."

"No, I don't want to put him in gaol. Can't be bothered with folks in there chattering all day. Dead bodies don't talk, I don't mind them, and they are in the back room," was the sheriff's reply.

They were standing outside the hotel, and Manuel indicated the sheriff's office. "We'll come and help you look through those wanted posters now," he said.

"No, no need. I'll do it. No need for anyone else to come." The sheriff's reply was brusque, and he strode away at a fast pace.

Both men watched the tall figure disappear into his office, the door firmly closed behind him. Josh looked at Manuel and raised an eyebrow.

"Yes, I think so too. Why doesn't our Preacher/sheriff want us to look through those wanted posters? And why don't we know the Preacher's full name? Strange, don't you think, Josh?" Manuel said.

"Maybe Parker isn't the only one with his face on a wanted poster," said Josh thoughtfully, looking at the closed door of the sheriff's office.

CHAPTER THIRTY-THREE

Amy and Josh were coming from Broken Horseshoe Ranch. She held the reins of her favourite horse, the elderly grey mare Bella, who was bringing them in on the buggy, for their day's work at the general store in Nowhere. They had just entered Main Street.

"The Devil! He's in Nowhere! This is the Devil's work. He'll lay waste to the town and everyone in it. Run, run, the Devil has come amongst us!" The wild shouts echoed down Main Street and ended in a horrific scream of terror.

"What's happening? What's going on?" Amy pointed to the crowd gathered around something lying in the middle of Main Street. "Can you see what it is?" Amy asked Josh, seated on the buggy beside her.

Taller than Amy, Josh hoisted himself up to see exactly what was at the centre of the crowd. "It's a dead chicken! They're standing around a dead chicken. And there are symbols drawn in the dirt."

Josh called over to Manuel, who was standing at the forefront of the crowd. "What's this all about, Manuel?"

Manuel walked over towards them. "It's a puzzle, Josh. Good morning, Amy," he greeted the girl as he replied to Josh.

A man standing nearby had heard Josh's question and rushed up to the buggy to tell the tale. "It's the Devil's work! Look at the chicken. It's been cut up and has Satan's mark on it. And it's not the first one that's been found like that." He was a skinny man, nicknamed Slim, who worked at the local saloon, and he loved to gossip. His long nose popped up and down with his agitated head as he gleefully recounted the rumours he'd heard.

Manuel pulled a face behind the man's back, for he was well known for his exaggerated stories. "There's some truth in that. It's not the first creature that has been seen mutilated, and there have been devil marks seen on barns and homes. Somebody is playing nasty tricks and using the Devil's name to scare people," said Manuel.

"It's not called Devil's Mountain for nothing. When people get possessed by the Devil, then we'll see whether or not Satan's coming back." The long-nosed man shook his head at Manuel's disbelief and trotted off to tell somebody else his dire warnings about the imminent arrival of the Devil to Nowhere.

Amy stared after him with a look of horror on her face. "That's rubbish, isn't it? Surely no one would kill and hurt a poor hen just to show the Devil's mark on it?" She looked at Manuel. "What do you think? You've lived in this area all your life. Have you heard of anything like this before?" Amy's snub nose screwed up in distaste, the many freckles across it joining together.

The shifting crowd moved, leaving a space through which Josh and Amy could see the chicken. The markings upon it were strange, and neither Amy nor Josh had seen anything like them before.

It took Manuel some time before he answered. "It's the Devil's Mountain. There have always been stories about strange happenings, unearthly beings walking along the cliff tops, and lights of a strange colour darting and flashing around the area. So, Amy, I just don't know. I go to church and I'm told not to believe in these things, but..." Manuel hitched up his baggy cotton trousers over his enormous belly, giving it a scratch. He straightened the suspenders holding them up, shook his head, and said to them both, "Let's get to work. Leave it to this lot to sort it out."

Turning away, they were moving towards the general store when further loud shouts erupted behind them. It was the skinny man again, and he was pointing to a tall Indian standing at the edge of the crowd. "It's them! He's one of those Indians who live on the edge of the Devil's Mountain. He's bringing the Devil into the town to make everyone in Nowhere mad. Clear off! Why wasn't he with the Navajo that Kit Carson sent away from Arizona? Indians shouldn't be allowed anywhere in Nowhere!" There arose a grumbling from the crowd, and several men turned towards the Indian with threatening gestures.

Josh moved restlessly beside Amy on the buggy. He made as if to get up and go towards the Indian to help him. But the Indian looked straight towards them both and shook his head slightly before slipping away. "I should have..." Josh began to speak to Amy.

But Amy whispered to him. "No, there was nothing you could do." Then she drove the buggy behind the general store and into the stable yard. "You saw Sam. He shook his head, he didn't want us involved. We can help him somehow, but not by making it plain how we feel about him," Amy whispered to Josh.

"He saved our lives, not once but twice. We owe Sam," insisted Josh.

"Sam shook his head. It was his signal to us. We mustn't show our friendship with him if he doesn't want us to," Amy said, but she wasn't happy about it. She was also remembering how Sam saved their lives, and it seemed dreadful that they could not speak out in his defence. However, Amy was sensible enough to realise the futility of arguing with an excited mob. No, they'd obey Sam's silent message and hope they could help him later. But it was sooner rather than later when Sam called upon them for their help.

CHAPTER THIRTY-FOUR

Amy jumped, startled when Sam silently appeared beside them in Manuel's small stable. He kept well back in the dark shadows and whispered. "I didn't want anybody to see us talking together. It's best that you don't acknowledge me when we're out and about in Nowhere."

"What's the matter? Sam, how can we help you?" Josh had finished settling Bella down in the stable and they were about to go into the general store to join Manuel. The tall Indian was standing there with a very sombre expression on his face. Usually, that face of his was inscrutable, and it was difficult to sense what emotion was beneath the surface, but not today. Sam was worried, and it showed!

"That man from the saloon has been shooting his mouth off. Talking rubbish about the symbols marked out in the dirt beside the dead chicken. And now new marks have appeared on the livery stable door," Sam said, folding his arms and hiding his emotions again behind his finely boned, sculptured face. His worry had been hidden away, and he now wore his usual masklike demeanour.

"What are the marks, Sam? And how do they affect you?" Amy said, touching his arm with a gentle pat. "Surely no one thinks you had anything to do with them?"

"Apart from the usual devil signs, there are other signs. These markings are like those of a maze, and very ancient. Many similar markings can be found all over the Devil's Mountain area and even all over this part of the country. The elders in our tribe say that they were made by those who built the cave dwellings in times past. Do you know of the cave dwellings?"

Josh and Amy exchanged glances, both remembering the ancient houses built halfway up the cliffs which they had encountered several days before. Neither had mentioned this area, or that they had visited it, to anyone, and both kept quiet now as their friend Sam spoke of them. Josh was thankful that Sam carried on talking, obviously unaware of their consternation at hiding this from him.

"The maze is a sign of magic, of black magic, so the elders tell us. It's not a complete circle, there is a break in it. This break leads to another world. The elders call it a portal." Sam looked at Amy and Josh, awaiting their thoughts on this strange story.

"Sam, before I arrived in Nowhere, I would have said that was utter rubbish." Josh's declaration was so abrupt that both Sam and Amy jumped, and then they both laughed. Josh continued, "I have been living here for some time now, and I can honestly say I would believe anything you tell me. Devil's Mountain is unique, as are its surrounding hills. They rise in steep jagged peaks, and there are deep hidden canyons and secret lost valleys with caves and many isolated desert springs. I can quite believe that there would be entrances to different worlds, but I don't want to find them or go there!"

"That's all very well," Amy was getting fed up with Josh rambling on. "What's all this got to do with you, Sam?"

"As you know, I've been working for some time in the livery stable and at the blacksmith's. I'm a fixture, and people hardly noticed me before. Now there is talk of the Indian trouble elsewhere, and looks have been cast in my direction, followed by an ominous silence. These remarks of Slim's now linking my tribe and family with the devil signs that are appearing have alerted people to my presence in Nowhere. I've become frightened that my family is in danger, so I'm going to move them tonight further up into the mountains, away not only from Nowhere but well away from the other Indian troubles. But it's the little one. It's a hard life, too difficult for a baby to survive." Sam paused, his eyes were pleading as he looked at Amy. He was too proud to ask her, but he hoped...

"Of course, we'll look after the baby! Some of my time is spent at the general store, but if you're happy for Nancy to take care of the baby, I know she'd love to have him. Would that be all right? I'll be there on weekends and most nights," Amy said. Sam nodded, the relief clear on his normally inscrutable face.

"I'm in your debt. You saved his life once before. I hoped you would do so again," Sam said.

"You saved our lives twice over, Sam. It's us that are in your debt," Josh said.

The Indian moved closer to Amy and looked down earnestly into her face. "Before I go, I have heard that your father is sick, Amy. Is it the lung disease?" His deep voice showed a care and concern unexpected by Amy, and his eyes grew warm as he looked at the girl.

Amy stared up at him, her eyes beginning to fill with tears. Luke was so ill now that they feared for his life. Most of the time he stayed in bed till lunchtime. Even then, it was an effort for him to get up and walk about during the afternoon before he went back to bed again. "Yes, Sam, he is so dreadfully ill, and it's his lungs. We all had the flu, my mother died and my father was left with damaged lungs. The doctor said dry air would help. But he's no better and is getting worse now."

A hand, burnt from his blacksmithing and calloused from his stable work, reached out and touched her arm gently. "I have a traditional medicine for him. A tiny spoonful of it each day may help him. It's an old medicine that has been used in my tribe for many generations for lung disease."

After that whispered remark to Amy, Sam vanished, leaving them both in the stable staring at one another.

"Is Sam really in danger? Surely the people of Nowhere don't think he's capable of black devil magic? I'm frightened, Josh. Our friends and neighbours are taking notice of these wild stories. Where will it lead to? How is it going to end?"

CHAPTER THIRTY-FIVE

A large wagon came each week delivering goods and mail to Nowhere. Owned by a merchant in Duloe, the nearest town with a postal service and regular stagecoach transport, the goods were transported for a fee. Manuel's dream was for a weekly stagecoach delivery to Nowhere, but the town was still too small for it to be profitable for a stagecoach company. It was still really a township, having only a few buildings that were permanently built and not with false wooden fronts and tents behind them. The collection of items thrown down from the wagon soon piled up on the boardwalk in front of the general store.

"Any post for me today?" Manuel asked the driver as usual. It was the regular joke that passed between them. Manuel never got any post addressed to him, but he took delivery of all the post and parcels for those living in Nowhere and the outlying districts. Manuel dealt with it, keeping some for his customers who would call in for it, and putting on one side those parcels and mail that he would take on his delivery days.

"Here's some old copies of the newspapers for you, Manuel. I know you like to read them even if the news is stale." The driver threw down the bundle of old newspapers tied with twine before he trundled off up to the livery stable, where the horses would be changed for the return trip. The wagon was given a perfunctory clean for those passengers who braved the jolting journey on its return to Duloe. When the fresh horses were saddled up, Sam brought the wagon to await the driver outside the general store. Manuel had mail and parcels ready addressed and sorted out to go east, and the hardy travellers knew to collect there for the journey back to Duloe.

"Time that driver had finished drinking in the saloon. One of these days, he'll be so drunk he'll fall off when they hit the roughest bumps of the journey. He's not meant to drink at all, let alone the whiskey and beer he puts away," grumbled Manuel.

The driver emerged from the saloon, wiping his mouth before putting on his gloves. Manuel stood with his arms folded and glared his disapproval. "I've loaded up the post and parcels for you, and you've got a couple of passengers sitting waiting inside. You shouldn't be drinking with that journey ahead of you."

His gloves were finally on, and the driver pulled his hat down low and shambled to the side of the wagon. He climbed up without saying a word to Manuel. The wagon finally trundled off, leaving the furious general store owner standing in a swirling cloud of dust.

Amy and Eliza were sorting out the packages on the counter. "Here's another one for the two Hobbs brothers. They always get these food parcels. At least I think it's food," Eliza said as she fingered the large parcel. "Feels like they have packets inside, and this one is some sort of grain." Eliza passed the parcel to Amy, after squeezing and shaking it.

"Yes, you're right. Do you think they have wheat posted from back east? Why would they do that?" Amy said, passing the parcel back to Eliza, who put it with the other packages needing to be delivered.

"There are special dried herbs and grain in that parcel. A relative sends it to the elder brother. It's a special family recipe for bread," Manuel told them as he joined them to see what had arrived. He put the papers on one side of the counter, ready to read at his leisure, but an advertisement caught his eye as he did so. "That crook! The swindling... well, I won't say the word I'd like to say in front of ladies. Look here, he's advertising land on the Thompson property as if it was luscious green grassy land, when it's nothing of the sort." His chubby, calloused finger pointed the advert out to the others, who gathered around him.

"Why, he makes it sound as if it's pasture land when it's nothing but desert and very little water," Amy said. "How could he? It's almost murder, having people come out to live in a desert area with no water and with no food easily grown." Amy's hand hovered over her Colt Peacemaker in her pocket, almost as if she'd like to put a bullet through the man.

"If only we could stop him somehow," Josh said. A smile crossed his lips as he looked at the indignant Amy. Her face was screwed up with fury, and her braids seemed to quiver in sympathy with her anger. Josh was delighted. The handsome, smooth-talking Charles Roberts had appeared in their lives showing a decided liking for Amy. Each time he met her, the flattering words that came from him caused Josh's hand to clench into a fist. And that fist itched to plant itself in the leering, smiling face of Charles Roberts.

"Amy! There's a letter here for Ben. Look, it's addressed to Ben Tanner, Broken Horseshoe Ranch, Nowhere. What's your young brother doing to get letters from somewhere out East? The writing is so poor, and it's smudged. I can't see what it is or where it's come from." Eliza lifted the envelope to the light as if it would help her see who the sender had been and where the letter had come from. She handed it to Amy, who also exclaimed over the unusual sight of her younger brother getting a letter. Turning it repeatedly in her hands, she walked to the back of the general store and into the private quarters to place it into her satchel. She gave the letter a last lingering look as she closed the flap of the satchel and returned to join the others.

"I don't think the Thompson place has been sold to Roberts," Manuel said. "I'm sure Preacher said they hadn't got a buyer yet."

"If it hasn't been sold, then how can Charles Roberts sell off the land if he doesn't own any?" a puzzled Amy asked.

"I don't know, but I think after we finish our deliveries for the day, Josh, I'm going down to have a chat with the Preacher about this advertisement and our friend Charles Roberts. Something has got to be done about that man to end his fraudulent plans," Manuel declared. "It's not only fraud but also a cruel deception. It could cost people their lives and all their savings. I can't stand by and let him go ahead with his despicable scheme!"

CHAPTER THIRTY-SIX

That day passed quickly for both Josh and Manuel. Everywhere they went, especially when they were delivering the goods to the outlying properties, questions were asked and speculation was rife about the Devil's return. The conversations ranged from wild, fanciful horror to stubborn disbelief. "I don't know about you, Josh. How does the gossip travel from one place to the next so quickly? I reckon it's blown in the wind. But it's never the facts, there's always something else added to it," Manuel said as they were returning from their last delivery.

Manuel's decision to deliver goods in return for produce from the homesteaders and ranchers had been a success. Not only was he welcomed, and the goods he delivered along with the post saved his customers from the journeys to Nowhere, which were long and arduous, but he in return was also assured of fresh produce to sell in the store.

"Who do you think's behind it all, Manuel? And why are they doing it? You don't believe it's the Devil, do you?" Josh asked. He had been deep in thought about Sam's problems and how this Devil business was affecting his friend. Now he realised he had only been listening with half an ear to Manuel's remarks and thought he should join in the conversation and perhaps get more information from his companion.

"I don't know," was Manuel's honest reply. "So far, it seems pretty harmless nonsense. But I am worried; there could be more to it. But what is behind it and who's doing it is something I don't understand. I don't believe it's the Devil."

There was an uneasy atmosphere over the small Main Street with its scattered buildings when they directed the wagon into it. The town of Nowhere had been named by the first person to arrive there. He'd said it was in the middle of nowhere. So Nowhere it became, and the folk living in and around it called it a town. It wasn't. But as in the way of all new frontier towns, it could grow up in a matter of months. The saloon was being rebuilt by Seth and his new partner. Zach had got the reward money for tracking down Parker, and he had previously worked as a bartender for Seth. Having no family, the saloon owner had been delighted to take Zach into the business. Zach was now a partner and put in his bounty to upgrade the saloon.

"Well, Josh, time for you to get home to Broken Horseshoe Ranch with Amy. As you have seen, we're getting busier each day. Think it over, but I would like you to have a chat with Amy and see if you both can consider coming in at least one extra day for me. Eliza is getting near the end of her pregnancy, and she's getting exhausted and appreciates Amy's help in the store. I'm also thinking of extending the store out further to house all the hardware. More people want shovels and other tools; especially now the silver mine is opening up on the other side of Devil's Mountain. I need the space to hold them. It's a growing business, Josh." Manuel stepped down off the wagon and looked up at Josh, who still sat thinking over Manuel's words. "Take your time, Josh, but consider my proposition. I know you've lost your memory and can't remember what you did before, but you have a choice facing you now. Do you stay and work at Broken Horseshoe Ranch? Or will you consider coming into the store and working with me? I could use a man like you who I know and trust. It would probably be full-time and you would have to consider living in Nowhere."

Whilst sorting out the horse and the wagon, Manuel cast worried looks at Josh as he silently helped the older man. Josh knew Manuel was wondering what his thoughts were about this proposition that he had sprung upon him. When they were coming out of the stable, Josh turned to Manuel. "Thank you for your offer, Manuel. I appreciate it, and if you will give me time, I'll think about it."

A beaming smile broke out on the Mexican's face, and he slapped Josh on the back. "That's all I can ask of you, Josh. Sleep on it. Take your time to make your decision."

The journey back home to Broken Horseshoe Ranch was becoming routine now, after each day's work at the general store for Josh and Amy. It was a time for them both to unwind and chat about the day's events. Bella, the grey mare, knew her way back and was always eager to return to the ranch. Most late afternoons there was increasing coolness in the air, which was welcome after working in the hot, dusty store, or in Josh's case, out on the buggy with the sun beating down upon him.

"What a day. It's hard to say what I think about it," Josh said, his voice betraying the puzzlement he felt at the peculiarities that morning had brought. "All that stuff about the Devil coming down from his mountain has to be rubbish, doesn't it?"

"I'm going to ask Ezra. He's lived in this area for many years. Both he and Leah lived in the cabin behind ours for some time before we arrived at Broken Horseshoe Ranch. If anyone knows if there's truth in it, Ezra will. I think it's somebody out to cause trouble, or just..." Amy's voice faded away as she realised herself, like Josh, she didn't know what to think about it.

They both had a lot to think about because, unknown to either of them, the Mexican couple had approached them individually. Amy and Josh had become invaluable to them, and Amy had been approached by Eliza to work the extra hours as well.

The heat of the day was fast evaporating, with a cool chill creeping over the ground. An approaching darkness of the night could be seen on the horizon as the sun dropped behind the jagged peaks of the mountains.

Bella needed no guidance, and she plodded along, her pace quickening, eager to get home. Then she paused slightly, her ears pricked up, and she looked to the side. They both followed her gaze and saw a figure standing there in the shadows.

"Who is it? What do they want?" Amy whispered.

The buggy had stopped. Bella stood patiently waiting, her ears pricked up as she looked at the stranger standing motionless in the shadows. Bella was unconcerned, almost as if she knew the person who had been waiting for them.

Josh slid his gun out of its holster and placed it on his lap, pointing it towards the figure. He had learnt since his arrival at Broken Horseshoe Ranch that one always had to be prepared and could never take a chance. Beside him, he felt rather than saw Amy also had her Peacemaker out from the hidden pocket of her skirt. Sighing with relief, he knew they were both prepared for whatever action the stranger would take.

"Who is it? Can you tell who it is?" Amy's voice was harsh with tension. "What do they want with us?"

CHAPTER THIRTY-SEVEN

Josh breathed out a sigh of relief. He hadn't realised that he was holding his breath until it all came out in a whoosh. "It's Sam and his family." The group stood silently in the shadow of the towering rocks. "Hello, Sam, you scared us for a moment."

The tall, muscular figure of Sam detached himself from the group, and an older woman walked alongside him as they approached the buggy. Sam carried a bag, whilst the woman took off the cradleboard, which had been on her back holding the baby. The fading light of the sun highlighted the decorative designs on the board itself. Lifting the child, she walked towards the buggy and held him up to Amy.

"This is the child. You promised to care for him. It was best that we gave him to you secretly. No one will know that he is one of ours," Sam said.

Holding out her arms, Amy took the baby and gazed down at the sleeping infant with a smile on her face. "He's grown," she whispered. Amy could see in the fading sunlight the tears trickling down the woman's face. "I'll look after him. Everyone at the ranch will take great care of him, I promise you this." Cradling the swaddled baby in her arms, Amy reached down and whispered again to the woman. "I promise you, we will take care of him."

The repetition of the words seemed to reassure the woman. A slim hand reached up to the child and gently stroked his face. As she did this, the woman's hair could be seen beneath the covering she wore, as it slipped from her head. A last ray of sunshine seemed to light up a few locks of hair that were visible, and both Amy and Josh could not mistake the greying blonde hair and the white skin of the woman.

Sam caught Josh and Amy's indrawn breaths of astonishment at the sight of the woman and gave a small smile. "My mother. Yes, she is a white woman. My family will go into the Hidden Valley. There, we will be safe and have time to think things over." His hand gestured towards the woman, and she gave them a sad smile. "Josh and Amy, you can see we have options we can take. We belong to neither community, not the Indian nor the white community. We will decide where we would find it best to fit in. For the care of the child, thank you." A gentle pat on the baby's head and Sam turned around and strode off into the darkness, his arm on the shoulder of the older woman who could be heard crying softly, the small group closing around them as they departed on foot.

The child slept all the way to Broken Horseshoe Ranch. Ben and Chan rushed out as usual to greet them and see to Bella and the buggy.

Amy put a finger to her lips as both boys were about to speak. "Hush, you'll wake the baby," Amy whispered as Josh came round to help her out from the buggy. She held the sleeping baby, hoping to keep him quiet. By that time, Nancy had appeared and stood on the porch, watching Amy climb up the steps, taking great care with the baby in her arms. Quick-witted Nancy took one look at the sleeping child and went back to hold the door open for Amy to enter the cabin. "My father?" Amy whispered.

"He's gone back to bed, but he had a better day. He tried to stay awake to wait for your return," Nancy whispered back, her face serious and sympathetic towards Amy.

Tom, Chan's older brother, stood at the stove, stirring a large pot. He smiled at Amy but continued with his stirring. Still a new arrival at Broken Horseshoe Ranch, he was doing his best to fit into the family group that had grown up around Luke, Amy, and Ben. Taller than his younger brother, he was still thin from his arduous journey to find his brother. He had an unpronounceable Chinese name when he arrived in America and had been given the name Tom by the miner who had bought him. So Tom he had remained, even though they offered to speak his Chinese name. But their pronunciation of it had both Chinese boys laughing uproariously, and they said it had become a rude word when they said it, and that they both preferred Tom.

Josh brought in the bag that Sam had given to him. He handed it to Nancy and went straight to the coffeepot sitting on the side of the stove. As he poured a cup for himself and one for Amy, Josh realised he had picked up Luke's coffee habit. Never seen without a cup of coffee in his hand, even drinking cold coffee, Luke seemed to survive on it. Sipping the bitter black taste of it, Josh thought to himself that he could have worse habits than constantly drinking coffee.

The child was still asleep and had been placed on a pile of quilts and blankets in the corner of the room. Nancy had produced a drawer from the bureau she had brought with her, now to be used for the baby. They all took their places at the table, and Tom placed bowls of a steaming stew in front of them with tiny dumplings. All of them stared at the bowls in surprise. The smell was unusual, and none of them had tasted tiny dumplings like those before. Tom stood with his hands clasped together as he watched and waited for the reactions to his cooking.

"That was delicious, Tom." Josh sat back with a sigh of contentment. It had been his second bowl, and he watched enviously as Amy finished up her second bowl. There was no more left. It had all been eaten. "What was in that? It was delicious."

It was Chan who answered. "My brother has used the herbs we have grown, and that was made from vegetables only. You liked it?" The proud face of Chan at his brother's skill in cooking made them smile.

Placing a spoon in the empty bowl, Amy smiled at the boys. "We loved it. Both of us having second helpings and..." Amy never finished her remark. A sudden wail from the corner made everyone turn to the child, who had woken up. It was a deafening wail and seemed to reverberate around the room. Luke emerged from his bedroom, his eyes wide in astonishment at the unexpected noise from the new occupant of the ranch.

CHAPTER THIRTY-EIGHT

They had placed the child in a wooden drawer from the bureau that Nancy had brought with her from Dry Creek Ranch. He had slept solidly since he had been given to Amy by Sam. Nestled in a pile of quilts, still swaddled in the clothes he had arrived in, he had not been disturbed by the new surroundings. Not until he woke with a sudden cry.

"Sam gave us a bag containing some of the baby's things. After his mother gave the baby to Amy, this was placed on our buggy." Josh handed the bag to Nancy, who placed it on the table and began to unpack it.

Meanwhile, Amy lifted the child and tried to hush his angry cries. A woven cloth bag with canvas straps held all the child's worldly goods. Nancy began taking everything out of the bag and placing it on the table.

Lifting the baby, Amy smiled at him. "Hello there. Do you remember me?" His loud cries stopped in surprise, and he stared at her as she cradled him in her arms. One chubby hand stretched up, grabbed one of Amy's braids, and tugged on it. It was a hard tug. "Ow!" exclaimed Amy, and tried to lessen the grip of those tiny fingers. "That hurt. You're a sturdy boy, aren't you?"

"There's a few pieces of cloth and a note here." Nancy pulled out of the bag the pitiful belongings of the child, some swaddling clothes, and a tiny rag doll, which had been homemade from various oddments of fabric. "One leg of this doll has been chewed again and again. It must be his favourite toy," said Nancy. She delved further into the bag and brought out a small brown bottle with a cardboard tag tied to it with string. The tag had some words crossed out, previously the name of a condiment, but on the other side it had the words "**1 teaspoon each day**" written in bold letters below Luke's name. "This is for you." Nancy handed Luke the bottle.

Josh leaned towards Luke to see the label. "Sam had that medicine made up especially for you, Luke."

"You will take it, won't you, Pa?" Amy, still nursing the baby, anxiously asked her father.

"What's it made of?" Luke asked and held the bottle up to the light, the better to see the contents.

"Sam mentioned herbs and roots of special plants, among other things. The recipe comes handed down from his grandfather's tribe," was Amy's reply.

The bottle was placed on the table by Luke. After coughing a few times, he held a handkerchief to his lips. As he took it away, he glanced at the cloth. It was bloodstained. Luke gave a deep sigh, screwed it up into a tightly wadded ball, and clenched it into his fist. "Don't worry, Amy. I'll take it."

Amy walked over to the table. She sat down with the child on her knee. He was silent. His gaze lingered from one strange face to the other.

Nancy delved into the very bottom of the bag and produced a brown paper note, torn from some old package and scribbled on. "I found a note. '*Thank you for taking care of him. He loves his doll. His name is David.*'" The note was handed around, and each person in the group stared at it.

"David? Strange name for an Indian?" Nancy said. "Sam is a strange name also, come to think about it."

"Both are biblical names. Perhaps the grandmother grew up in a home of God-fearing Christians before she was captured by Indians," said Luke.

"Why didn't she escape when they were near

Nowhere?" Ben scratched his head, thinking about the problem the woman had faced.

"And leave her family? Leave her children and grandchildren behind? And where would she go? And how would she live? No, Ben, she was better staying where she was, for the moment," Nancy said.

"Let's take this bonnet thing off your head." Amy removed the tight-fitting cap from the child's head. "Oh, my goodness!" Amy exclaimed.

Gasps of astonishment escaped from every one of them.

CHAPTER THIRTY-NINE

Amy reached out with a trembling finger towards the child's curls. "It's blonde, his hair is blonde!" The silky strands of hair became entwined in her fingers, and Amy gazed wide-eyed at it. "But when we had him before, when he was just born, it was just a fuzzy brown covering on his head. I expect that grew out, and this has appeared."

Ezra stroked his beard, his rheumy eyes focused on the child's head, and he screwed them up to see the blonde curls better; almost as if to change exactly what his eyes were telling him he saw. "Whoever heard of a yellow-haired Indian?" He shook his head, "that's a new one on me."

"Sam's mother. Did you see her, Amy? I thought she wasn't an Indian. This child would be her grandson. Perhaps he gets the fair hair from her," Josh said and turned to Amy for confirmation.

"Her hair was tightly covered, but when her head covering slipped and I saw greying blonde hair, then..." Amy began speaking but was interrupted by an excited Josh.

"Blonde hair! She's also got hair like the baby." Josh jumped to his feet at this fresh and startling development in their friendship with the Indians. "And, Amy, have you looked at Sam's hair? Really looked at it?"

Amy shook her head. She had begun to remove the child's outer layers and was engrossed in her task. "No, why? It's dark brown, isn't it?" She replied absent-mindedly, struggling, as the boy was waving his arms around wildly and was intent on catching hold of her braids again.

"Amy, I noticed before that Sam's hair has roots that are lighter than the rest of his hair." Josh began pacing the room, as his thoughts – jumbling about in his mind – took shape and began to make sense. "Blonde, or as Ezra says, yellow. I think Sam has yellow hair and dyes it brown in keeping with the other Indians in his tribe."

A thoughtful silence fell on the room as everyone digested these remarks from Josh. It was Luke who spoke first, after he reached out and patted the curly-headed child. David had finally captured Amy's braid and was chewing contentedly on its end. "No wonder Sam speaks English. Perhaps that's why he doesn't have tribal markings on him. The poor fellow is neither Indian nor a white man. In times like these, where does he go? And what colour will he decide to be, and at best be only tolerated by that group he's aligned himself with? Poor Sam, no wonder he's taking his family away into the hills. He has a decision to make. I wonder what decision that will be? Will he follow the other Indians from his tribe onto a reservation? Or will he try to become a white man?"

The next morning, Amy and Josh set off for their work in Nowhere. At the porch stood the two women with baby David. Nancy was holding him, with Leah casting envious eyes upon her.

"Do you think they will come to blows over the baby?" Josh said, as they waved goodbye and Bella set off down the track leading out of the ranch. Josh flicked his hair back off his face. It was longer than ever, and so bleached now by the sun to be almost white. His hair was untameable and had always been difficult to get cut properly. Josh had dodged Ezra when he'd noticed him hacking Ben's, Chan's, and Tom's hair. He was hoping to pluck up the courage to beg Eliza to cut his hair. Manuel's hair always looked neat, and Josh eyed it enviously.

"I hope David will be all right. It's such a different lifestyle for him," said Amy. "And so many strange faces, unusual food tastes and..."

Josh interrupted her. "That baby is being pampered and spoiled, fed and cared for every minute of the day. It's a better lifestyle for him than to be traipsing up canyons and the peaks of the Devil's Mountain. Another reason Sam didn't want the child with them was for the entire group's safety," Josh said.

"The group's safety?" Amy turned to Josh with surprise at this remark.

"If they are pursued by people hostile to them or any predator, such as a bear or a lion, a crying baby could give their hiding place away. And, Amy, I think you'll agree, that baby has a powerful set of lungs!" Josh said.

"That's so true! My head is still ringing from his cries last night," said Amy. "But, Josh, I have heard that some Indian tribes train their babies to keep silent and not cry. I don't think anyone could train David to keep quiet, though." Amy gave a gurgle of laughter at the very thought of trying to keep the baby David quiet.

Josh glanced at the girl beside him. Her laughter was rarely heard now. Her father's illness, the recent difficulties, and the deaths that they had faced all contributed to Amy's increasing solemnity. He liked to see her laugh, the way her smile crinkled the corners of her eyes and her freckles seemed to dance across her face. If only he could make her laugh more often.

It was a tired pair that drove into the stable yard behind the general store. Automatically, they dealt with

Bella and climbed the stairs to the back door. Josh had already seen that the wagon was partly loaded. Manuel had been busy already. The deliveries were mounting up as more people moved into the area. Josh could see that it was going to be a busy day. He didn't know how busy and difficult that day would be!

CHAPTER FORTY

"We've got a lot of deliveries today. I think it's going to be a long, hard one, Josh," Manuel said, and he handed some boxes to Josh before he picked up more himself. "I couldn't manage without you. In fact, the increased work at the store is getting almost as much as Eliza and I can cope with." They struggled out with the boxes, the small brown paper packages, and the few breakable items that somehow Manuel usually carried precariously on top. Always, Eliza shook her head at his method of transporting the goods. Always, she was certain that he would drop something and break it, but to Josh and Amy's amusement, Manuel never did. No matter how wobbly the packages were, they always arrived safely in the wagon.

Out of the stable yard and out onto Main Street, the wagon drove past the general store. Both Manuel and Josh waved at Amy, who was sweeping the boardwalk preparatory for the first customers. Overnight, the ever-present dust of the desert landscape would swirl into town and lie in piles of dust and debris. Eliza was straightening vegetables in the front window and she, too, smiled as the men drove past. Amy entered the store to the back, where she continued sweeping. She turned as two men clattered into the store. Holding the broom, she paused, standing still, eyeing the men uncertainly.

Eliza looked up from behind the counter. "Good morning. Can I help you?" She asked them.

Both men laughed at this remark. "Oh, yes, you can help us!" One man closed the door behind him and turned the key in the lock. He reached up and turned the open sign hanging on the back of the door to the closed one.

They both walked with heavy footsteps into the store. "Looking forward to some help." The older, bald one laughed at this remark, his sly eyes darting everywhere around the store.

Amy tightened the grip she had on the broom handle, whilst her other hand moved into the hidden pocket in her skirt. The men were dirty and unshaven, with scraggly beards, and they moved into the store with a purposeful air. They weren't going to buy anything, Amy realised that. They were going to take what they could and no payment would be offered. All Amy could hope for was that she and Eliza would be alive when they left.

The older of the two, a burly man with a scar running down his cheek, stood there with his gun in a calloused hand. His eyes darted around the store, looking for valuables and supplies to pilfer, necessities for their journey to the silver mine on the other side of the Devil's Mountain. Both of the miners' faces were lined with the evidence of the hard lives they led, and the desperation within their eyes and the avid greed with which they looked around the store were frightening to both women.

"Get some sacks, woman, and start putting these provisions in them." Eliza moved along the counter and placed a couple of sacks on top of it. She gave a sideways look at Amy, which warned her not to cause any trouble but to wait. Amy realised Eliza was standing beside the hidden gun beneath the counter, which was always kept ready for such emergencies. But for the moment, Eliza began putting packets of coffee, beans, flour, and other provisions that were handed to her into the sacks.

"We need those shovels and pickaxes for when we get to the mine. Best take them from here, Curly. They'll cost too much over there at the mine," said the older man. The other, younger, man, who was wearing a tattered shirt beneath a stained vest, nodded at the older man and began grabbing tools from the hardware section of the store.

So that's what they were, Amy realised. They were on their way to the silver mine that had recently discovered a new vein of silver ore. On the far side of the Devil's Mountain, the excitement of this fresh discovery of silver had brought a flood of people into the area. Some had come through Nowhere, finding the small collection of the general store, the saloon, the hotel, and the few houses on their way to join the rush of silver prospectors. That explains the scuffed boots and the general air of dirtiness, Amy thought. They are miners. She moved closer to Eliza, and in so doing, the younger one caught sight of her for the first time.

"Never mind these shovels. I fancy this pretty girl. Why, isn't she a beauty?" He walked over to Amy, looking her up and down, mentally undressing her as he did so. Amy's jaw tightened, and she clenched her hands, trying to keep calm and not lose her temper. Amy would have loved to have screamed insults at him. But she knew better than to antagonise him. So Amy said nothing.

"Cat got your tongue? Nothing to say for yourself? All the better; can't stand a caterwauling woman. Let's you and I have some fun back here." He stepped forward and reached out a grubby hand. An overwhelming stench surrounded him: of unwashed clothes and a sweat-stained body. His breath smelt, even at this early time in the morning, of alcohol, the fumes making her want to retch.

"No, thank you, just get what you want and leave," Amy said, her quiet voice masking the inward fear and trembling of the girl. And the rising anger. Amy edged away from him, nearer to Eliza.

"No, thank you! No, thank you!" The younger man slapped his thigh and laughed uproariously as he mimicked her voice.

"Leave her be, Curly. Let's just get the goods and get out of here. Don't be stupid and start messing with the girl. Got you into trouble before, didn't it? You always have to mess with the women." The older of the two men didn't stop his actions in grabbing provisions and piling them onto the counter as he shouted at the younger one. "Stupid fool! Stealing provisions means nothing. Attacking a young girl will have the whole town after us. Don't be a fool, Curly, get grabbing all the stuff that we'll need."

Curly swung around and glared at his partner. "That's too many times you've called me stupid. The last person who called me a fool ate his words along with my bullet. If I want to have a bit of fun with this girl, that's my business. Ain't nothing to do with you!" His hand hovered over his gun holster.

CHAPTER FORTY-ONE

The older man grabbed a tin kettle and tin plates from a shelf, throwing them onto the counter, ignoring the din it made when they landed on the wood. Stuffing them into a canvas bag, he yelled over his shoulder. "All I'm aiming to do is get me to that mine before all the silver runs out! Time enough to enjoy a woman or two when we have silver in our pockets. Leave her be, Curly. Grab the gear that we'll need when we get to the mine. Hurry, anyone could come to the store and look in the window." The older man turned away and lifted a couple of the bags that Eliza had filled. But as he did so, he muttered under his breath, "Stupid young fool..." Those were the last words he ever uttered.

The gunshot sounded loud in the general store, and the smell of the recently fired gun hung in the air. Curly held the gun in his hand as he looked down at his former partner. "Didn't I warn you? Didn't I tell you not to call me stupid? Shot my old man for calling me that when I was ten years old. Didn't take it from him and sure enough not gonna take it from you." He laughed uproariously. His manic laughter seemed to echo around the general store, bouncing off the wooden floorboards and walls.

The women were transfixed, both too frightened to move after that deafening sound of the unexpected gunshot. Neither of them could take their eyes away from the man on the floor, the blood slowly oozing from his head, his limbs contorted as he fell. Surreptitiously, Amy fingered her Colt Peacemaker in her pocket. She readied it for action. Standing, as she was, behind and to the side of the counter, she saw with approval Eliza's hand gripping a gun beneath the counter.

For a moment, Curly stood looking down at his former friend. His laughter had stopped, and he looked puzzled as he realised what he had done. Without a partner, he was going to find life difficult, working alone to mine for the silver. Shrugging, he walked over to the body and gave it a kick in the ribs. "Serves you right. Thought we were partners. I'm not gonna take orders from anyone." Then he reached for the sacks of provisions. Realising that there was a lot to carry for just one man, he looked at Amy.

Eliza followed his glance and looked stricken as she realised his intentions. She manoeuvred the gun until it was just beneath the counter, pointing at Curly. But he moved, and now Amy was in her line of fire. Eliza had no clear line of sight. She couldn't shoot him now because Amy was in the way.

"Can't carry all this stuff myself. He's dead and useless. You look like a pretty strong girl. Fancy I'll take you along with me. You can help me carry this lot, and we can have a little fun on the way." Again, he looked Amy up and down, licking his lips and leering at her.

"Leave me alone! Get out of town while you can. We'll give you a head start and not raise the alarm until you've left town," Amy said, her voice trembling. She was angry and yet too frightened to act. Curly was so wild in his speech and actions.

"No need for that," he said. He lifted the gun he was holding and pointed it straight at Eliza. "Once she's dead, there will be no one to give an alarm."

Another shot rang out in the general store. Again, smoke from a gun wreathed in the air, whilst the acrid smell lingered. Curly fell to the floor beside his erstwhile companion. Amy placed her gun on the counter and rushed to Eliza's side, clinging to the older woman. "I thought for sure he was going to shoot you! I just prayed my shot would reach him first," Amy said between sobbing gasps of relief.

Amy and Eliza clung to one another. Amy gently pushed the older woman onto a chair, fearing that she might have suffered harm after the upset, and mindful of her growing bulge. Banging and shouting at the doors alerted Amy to the fact that there were people outside, eager and anxious to find out what was going on.

"You all right, Eliza? Shall I let them in? I see the sheriff out there." At Eliza's nodding reassurance, Amy carefully walked around the two bodies sprawled on the general store floor and the spreading pool of blood. She grimaced at the sight and smell of the blood.

"What's been going on here? Are you two ladies hurt?" The sheriff, Lance Grey, who was also Nowhere's Preacher, pushed past Amy with his long stride. But he stopped, appalled at the sight that met his eyes. "Dead! Two men dead! What happened here? Eliza, ma'am, are you all right?" The sheriff bent over Eliza, resting a hand on her shoulder as she sat in the chair. Amy, still shocked, struggled to contain the giggles that she felt were about to erupt from a throat so dry from the tension.

It was Eliza who explained to the sheriff/Preacher, and it was Eliza who explained to the others who came into the store, eager to hear all about the occurrence. "I'm fine, just shocked. It was so very frightening, but Amy saved me," Eliza said, mopping her brow and face with a handkerchief. The hand that held it still shook a little. Eliza had grown up in a tough Mexican town where violence was the norm, not an unusual occurrence. But how close she had come to death in the last few moments had shocked her, and it was taking time for her to calm down after it. "I think I'm fine."

CHAPTER FORTY-TWO

"And you, miss Amy? How are you?" Grey had been joined by a few others crowding into the general store, eager to see what had occurred, and keen to find everything out to relate the lurid details to their friends later. Far from being frightened after her horrible experience, Grey was amazed to find a young girl standing before him, frowning over the burnt hole in her skirt.

"Didn't have time to get the pistol out of my pocket. Had to shoot him before he shot Eliza. He was about to fire at her. Now look what's happened. I've ruined my best skirt." At the sheriff's indrawn gasp of surprise at her remark, she looked up at him. "What? I don't have many skirts. Nuisance ruining it over some pesky, bushwhacking..." Amy stopped speaking. She realised she should weep and wail in the eyes of the watching men. To her relief, one of the original settlers to the settlement that was proudly called the town of Nowhere marched in the front door of the general store.

"Out of my way! Stupid men, let me get to Eliza. Sheriff, get going and do your duty. Get these dead men out of here! Not hygienic having dead men lying all about the place; especially a general store with provisions and suchlike." A plump, little lady, she bustled into the store, always dressed in black bombazine after the death of her husband. No one ever knew what had happened to the husband. Some people wondered if there had been a husband. But no one dared ask. The diminutive little lady had a sharp way about her, but a heart of gold. She was a midwife and nurse to most of the women in the surrounding area. Mrs Jones, or Dora as she was often called, was a force to be reckoned with in the town of Nowhere. "Don't want to know what happened here, just want to get you to your bed. Need to rest after a shocking incident like this, my dear."

Ignoring Eliza's protests at leaving the store unattended but for Amy, and how she needed to be on call all day as her husband was delivering goods to the outlying ranches, Dora had Eliza up and walking towards the back quarters where she and Manuel lived. "Miss Amy, you're a capable lass. Can you cope with the store today? I'll find someone to help you after I sort out Eliza here."

Relief flooded through Amy. She had been worried about her friend. Eliza had gone extremely pale after the last robber had been shot. A strong and capable woman, but she had been facing death at the end of a gun barrel, and Eliza was nearing the end of her pregnancy. Amy felt so grateful that Dora had appeared on the scene. Looking after the general store would be so much easier than coping with a pregnant woman.

Dora had disappeared with Eliza, but her words had not gone unheeded. The sheriff directed a few men to remove the two bodies to the sheriff's office, where there was a room at the back for dead bodies. Amy remembered that the last dead body to inhabit that room had been a vicious stalker. Determined to kill Josh, and also Amy as well, it had been Eliza who had saved them by shooting the stalker dead.

The men had gone with the sheriff, who had told Amy that he would come later to speak to her and Eliza about the events that had just taken place. A silence crept over the general store as the last of the sightseers left, and Amy shivered as she looked down at the bloodstains on the floor. She hadn't realised that blood had a strong smell. Amy shuddered. Skirting around them, she walked to the doors and locked them again, putting up the closed sign.

Amy looked down at the floor that she had freshly scrubbed. There was a dark mark, but she had got the worst of it out. She had replaced the provisions in their rightful places from the discarded sacks that had lain on the counter. The tools that Curly had been grabbing before he had attacked her, she picked up one by one and put them back also in their rightful places. Amy sighed and looked around the store. It was all back to its usual tidy condition, with everything back in its rightful place, as it should be. She took off the large apron she had borrowed from Eliza's hook and looked down at it. The dirt and the blood from the floor had covered it with unsightly and unpleasant marks. She screwed the apron up in a ball, took it through to the kitchen, and placed it ready for washing. Filling the coffeepot up, she put it on ready to brew. Edging closer to the bedroom door, she could hear the voices of Eliza and Dora still talking. Amy smiled to herself, pleased to hear Eliza sounding better, and turned to go back into the store.

When the coffee had brewed, Amy poured herself a large, strong tin cup and took it to the counter. She set it down after she'd had one sip of it, then walked purposefully to the doors, unlocked them, and turned the sign to open. Smoothing down her skirt, Amy gave a sad sigh again at the bullet hole. She went back to the counter and was about to lift her coffee for another drink when she realised that the store was becoming crowded. Some inhabitants of Nowhere must have been lurking outside, eager to come in to see the sight of the double deaths and to find out the story of how all the drama had unfolded from Amy and Eliza.

Amy took a deep breath. If truth be told, she would rather shoot down another bandit than face these eager time-wasters. But Eliza was counting on her; there was no way she could let her down. True, Eliza was her employer, but to Amy, she was more than that. She was her friend, and Amy would do anything to help the woman who had been so kind to her. Taking a deep breath, Amy went behind the counter and pasted a false smile on her face as she greeted the first customer. She dealt, lightly and without complaining, with the first two women, who were eager to find out everything that had happened that morning. She gave them an edited version, which didn't please them, so they left unsatisfied without the dramatic hysteria they thought Amy should be enacting.

Dora came from the back of the store, where Manuel and Eliza had their private quarters. She came behind the counter to stand beside Amy. "I've made Eliza rest. She needed to after that dreadful experience. You'll get lots of folk in this afternoon, eager to see and hear everything that happened this morning. I can see that you are coping well now, but you'll need help later. I know just the person. They'll be here in a few minutes."

She gave the girl a gentle pat on the back. "Well done, girl, for someone new to the Western way of life, you're doing well. Got to shoot the varmints when we find them. Both rats and men! You got that right, girl! Shoot the varmints, men and rats!"

CHAPTER FORTY-THREE

"Nearly home," sighed Manuel. It had been a hard day. Somehow, everyone wanted to chat with them, holding up their journey back to Nowhere. The Grangers, hospitable as always, were desperate to know everything that had happened concerning the Devil's marks on the mutilated chicken and the dirt of Main Street. They also had more stories about the Thompson homestead and the adjoining ranch, telling of further weird activities. Both ranches had been plagued by the devilish activities. With great difficulty, they escaped from the chatty couple.

"I enjoy the coffee, and especially the cake Mrs Granger makes. But how her husband can talk and talk? Josh, what do you make of his story about old Mr Thompson? He's had it worse than anyone. From what we've heard, he's having lights, eerie noises, and devil marks being drawn all over his ranch and even on the homestead walls themselves. Why is Mr Thompson being targeted in this way?" Manuel said.

"Yes, but it's not only old man Thompson, it's that ranch next to his as well. Do you know that property, Manuel? It's the first time I've heard of it," was Josh's reply.

The sun was getting lower in the sky, but it was still hot for the time of year. Both Manuel and Josh had set off early that morning, intending to arrive home earlier following the day's deliveries. However, there seemed to be a growth in people using Manuel's delivery service, and the carrier from Duloe found it increasingly lucrative to drop off essential mail packages for Manuel to deliver. Manuel took his time before replying to Josh.

"Originally, the Thompson property and the Brooks

property were joined with the Grangers and were in one extensive property owned by a Mexican family. When the father died, it was sold off, because no one wanted such an enormous property, so it was split up into three smaller ones. The Grangers have land reaching down to the Avon River, so even in a drought, they have ready access to water," Manuel told Josh as they drove along, their dust trail lengthening behind them.

"I imagine that's why the Grangers bought that property. They needed water, and plenty of it to irrigate Mrs Granger's flower garden," Josh said, smiling at the recollection of the woman's great pride and joy in her flowers.

"Fancy wasting water on flowers! The old saying around here is that water is the greatest treasure of all, not gold or silver. Just as well those Grangers have got money. No one else can afford to waste time and money on silly flowers. Most folk around here eke out a living planting vegetables and having small animals, just enough to be self-sufficient." Manuel shook his head at the folly of Mrs Granger. Then he wriggled about on the wooden seat of the wagon – easing his fat bulk, scratching his belly again, and pulling the baggy canvas trousers he always wore into a more comfortable position. "Old man Thompson bought that ranch without realising it lacked water. When he came to visit it before he put down his money, there was a well. But it only comes after the monsoon rains. That's when Thompson came to look at the property. Of course, it was full and overflowing then, but when the hot season comes, it dries up. That first year, when he realised the problem with the lack of water, he put it on the market, and he's been trying to sell it ever since."

Josh, too, squirmed about on the seat. After many hours of travelling on the wooden seat, it became harder each mile they travelled. Long-limbed and slim-hipped, he almost envied the plentiful bulk that Manuel had to sit on. Almost. He only hoped that, when he reached Manuel's age, he would not get so fat. "What about the other ranch? What was that property like?" he asked Manuel, continuing his train of thought.

"Again, like the Grangers', it has easy access to water. There is a small river running down from the foothills of the Devil's Mountain through their property, reaching the larger river Avon, which travels on to the Grangers'. If it was joined with old man Thompson's land, there would be water enough for both properties."

The conversation, as they drove along the last few miles of their journey, petered out between the men. But it was with renewed energy that the horses, Josh, and Manuel saw, in the distance, the buildings of Nowhere.

"We earned that beer tonight, Josh. Some days it's not so tiring, but somehow today has been a bad one. I'm parched and will be pleased to down a couple of beers," Manuel said.

A rider approached them, coming out of Main Street as they turned into it. "Hey there, Manuel. You're all right, are you? You're not dead? Thought you were the man that got shot." It was Slim, the thin, weedy-looking man who was always telling exaggerated stories and causing trouble with his barbed remarks about people. "Quite a shootout in the general store today," he said and rode on.

At first, Manuel turned to look after the figure. Manuel was about to shout for him to stop and to explain his remarks. But instead, he picked up the reins, shouted at the two horses, and drove them in a wild gallop towards the general store. Normally, he drove the wagon around the back to the stable. Not today. The reins were flung over the rail in front of the store. Manuel threw himself off the seat, his feet thundering a tattoo on the boardwalk as he rushed to the door. Speedy as Manuel was, Josh overtook him on the boardwalk, reached the door, and flung it open. "What's happened? Who got shot? Who was killed?"

CHAPTER FORTY-FOUR

Both entrance doors into the general store were flung back by the agitated men rushing from the buggy. The crash they made as they rebounded in front of the store windows made those inside jump and whirl around in surprise.

Manuel, in one bound, reached his wife and kissed her soundly, before taking both her hands and pumping them up and down. All the while, he was shouting, "You're alive! Eliza, you're alive. I thought you were dead."

"Yes, thank you. I'm alive. We both are, but who told you we were dead? How did you come to hear that story?" Eliza answered and smiled at him, but Manuel could see present in that smile the trauma that she had suffered earlier. Her face was drawn into lines, and she had lost her usual rosy complexion and was whiter than normal.

Manuel answered for both of the men. "It was Slim. He was riding out of Nowhere as we drove in. He told us that there had been gunfire in the store and that there were two people killed. But he didn't know who they were." Manuel, his arm around his wife, gave her a gentle hug as he looked down at her, almost as if he couldn't believe that she was there in person and not dead.

"That man takes a small story and blows it up into a huge, dramatic one," Eliza said, shaking her head at the folly of the man.

"Yes, there was gunfire, and yes, there were two dead in the store this morning. Thankfully, it wasn't us." Amy's voice told the story in a flat, emotionless tone. She continued unpacking the parcel that had arrived with goods for the general store. Each item she unwrapped, she concentrated on placing with infinite care in its correct position on a shelf.

Josh stared at Amy. Like Manuel, he too had raced into the store, fear overwhelming him. Fear that it was Amy who was dead. He had come to a halt in front of her. It was almost as if he was seeing her for the very first time. Her tiny snub nose and those freckles that marched across it and her cheeks were all so familiar to him. She wore her long brown hair tied into a couple of braids or just tied back loose and hung down to her waist. As usual, she loved to shrug herself into her favourite brown suede jacket, and the only feminine quirk she possessed was her fondness for different coloured bandannas.

"You're not hurt? What happened?" The two questions he asked were automatic reflexes from him. "Amy, you're all right then?" Josh couldn't help himself. He stepped forward and grabbed her and pulled her towards him. For a moment, he allowed himself the luxury of burying his head in her hair. The lingering scent of the herbs she used to rinse the long tresses seemed to flood into his mind. He could no longer fool himself. That awful thought – that she might be dead and gone from him forever – pushed all doubts away. Josh admitted the overwhelming fact to himself. He loved Amy, and it was not a passing fancy. Fearing that she might be dead had shown him the depth of his love and how life would be unbearable without her.

"Yes, Josh, we are both safe and unhurt. It was frightening for a moment, because one man was so wild and didn't seem to know what he was doing. Thankfully, we survived, but my skirt didn't do so well. I shot a hole in the pocket!" Amy looked down at the skirt and fingered the hole her gun had made as she had shot the wild intruder.

His hands went to her shoulders, and he pushed her back from him gently. Shaking his head at how Amy always belittled her actions and focused her attention on the silliest things, Josh laughed. "I'm sure you'll get a new skirt soon. In the meantime, can't you put a fancy patch on it?" The realisation of his love he buried deep within his heart. This loss of memory he had suffered ever since he had been attacked and left for dead in the desert meant he couldn't, in all honesty, tell her how he felt. What if a girlfriend was waiting for his safe return somewhere? What if there was even a wife, and here Josh cringed mentally, even children? No, he had to remain the good friend Amy believed him to be. She cared for him, Josh knew that. But to have her loving him? He wouldn't think about that. There was no way he would go down that road to find out what her feelings were for him. No, he wouldn't think about it.

"What a good idea, Josh!" Bending her head down to put her hands in both pockets and stretching out her skirt material, she gazed at each pocket. "I could do a matching pocket patch! Thank you, Josh." She raised her head straight up to him, with a grateful smile, but the smile faltered as if she was aware of those feelings he was trying so hard to hide. A long moment stretched between them as both looked at each other. Really looked at each other.

The moment was broken when Dora came into the room, looking around.

"Here he is. There's nothing Zach can do in the saloon at the moment. It's a real mess over there with men working on the building at the back of the main rooms. Seth told me that this fellow, Zach, is useless, getting in the way, and being a downright nuisance." The black bombazine dress Dora always wore rustled and swished towards them. "So he's here. He's going to help in the store in the mornings, and then in the saloon afternoons and evenings. Seth is managing tomorrow to get at least part of the room ready for those drunken idiots he serves. I can come in the afternoons on delivery days. No use with a gun, but I can scream and make a fuss that will put any robber off his game!" With that remark, Dora moved the tobacco she was still chewing in her mouth and spat it out in the spittoon Manuel always kept in front of the counter. The spittoon gave a loud noise and wobbled as her chew hit with her unerring aim.

"Told you I'd find someone to help. You can always rely on Dora! Not sure how much use he will be, but he's a good lad and willing." A hearty slap on Zach's back had him staggering across the floor, only steadying himself by clutching the counter as he fell forward.

Dora shook her head, smiled round at everyone, and stomped out of the general store with her usual rustling of skirts.

CHAPTER FORTY-FIVE

That had been a special moment when Josh and Amy were in the centre of the general store. Josh had dashed into the store and found Amy. She wasn't dead. Josh couldn't believe how wonderful that had felt. In that moment – when joy and relief flooded across his face as he looked at her – all the love he felt for her was clear in that fleeting moment. It had seemed a motionless minute they were trapped in, only seconds really, but it seemed to last forever as they both stared into each other's eyes with no defences up. Normally, all feelings were masked with the everyday glitter of the shields that both wore, keeping their emotions deep within their minds and hearts. But for that second, there were no defences up, no guards to hide the true reality of their feelings. Then it was gone.

"Thank you for saving my wife, Amy." Manuel's voice broke through to Josh and Amy. She blushed as Josh looked away, and she began smoothing her skirt, also looking away from everyone. Josh's colour was slightly heightened, but as he was tanned with the sun, especially from those long delivery treks with Manuel, it wasn't noticeable.

"You cleared up..." Eliza's voice came to a sharp stop, and she realised the enormity of what she was about to say. Taking a large gulp, she looked down at the floor. "Well done, Amy. I wasn't looking forward to clearing that up, but you did a great job here, and I can see that you must have sorted out all the provisions." She walked forward, put her arm around the girl, and kissed her on the cheek. "Thank you, Amy, for saving my life."

"I always pay my debts. You saved my life the other week!" Amy laughed. "That man was unpredictable and would have killed me in the end as well, so it is best he went when he did." Her last remark was a sober realisation of exactly what Curly had planned to do with her. "Yes, I had to get rid of him for both of our sakes."

Silence fell on the general store as each one of them gazed down at the newly scrubbed floorboards in the ominous shape of two men shot to death. It was broken by the loud shouting of a man outside on Main Street.

"Help me! Help me. The Devil has come to our ranch! He has possessed Ruth and Dorcas. Where is Dora? Can anybody help me? Where is the Preacher? He must pray over them and remove the Devil!" The clatter of buggy wheels and the abrupt halt of the horses sounded loud in the sudden quiet that his shouting had caused in Main Street. Everyone came running to see what was amiss. Manuel rushed outside the store onto the boardwalk with Josh beside him. Everyone erupted from the saloon, the livery stable, and the blacksmith's. There was quite a crowd gathered round the elder Hobbs brother, and the two women seated beside him on the buggy.

All eyes were upon them except for Josh's. There it was again. That tingle was on the back of his neck. It only came when someone was watching him. Since his arrival at Broken Horseshoe Ranch, it had occurred several times. Only when someone was watching him. He looked at the buggy and the two women, and then his eyes flickered towards the crowd that was gathering around and looking with great interest at the buggy and its occupants. Josh knew that not everybody was looking at the buggy. No, someone was looking at him. For some reason, they had no interest in the buggy and its occupants. Their interest was fully occupied with watching him.

Amy had joined him. She felt the increasing tension of Josh as she came up beside him. His eyes were not upon the spectacle in front of them. She watched as Josh scanned the crowd. He moved further along the boardwalk, to see over all the crowd. "What is it, Josh? What's the matter?"

"Someone is watching me. I felt it, and it's happened a few times lately. I think it's the same man. He has a distinctive birthmark on his face. He's tried to hide it with huge whiskers and a beard. It's quite obvious: over his nose. He always wears a large, dirty canvas coat in a beige colour, no matter what the weather. It looks as if it belonged to a bigger man. I've seen him several times lately," Josh answered her, speaking in a soft voice so that the others would not hear.

"You think it's another killer? Someone else sent to murder you? The masked rider tried hard to kill you first, then there was the other stalker. Now you think there's someone else in Nowhere eager to see you die? When will it ever end? Who is this man called Duke? Why does he want you dead? Whatever happened to you before you lost your memory? Why did it merit someone chasing you and paying time after time for men to kill you?" Amy's angry questions fell on deaf ears because Josh had spotted the man who was watching him.

"I've had enough of this endless watching me. I'm going to get him, and, if I have to, I'll choke the truth out of him!" Josh leapt over the hitching rail down onto the dusty street and raced round the back of the crowd towards the man. The man's eyes widened as he saw Josh race towards him, and Amy could see he took a deep breath because those enormous whiskers quivered before he set off to run around the back of the crowd, away from

Josh's approach.

In seconds, Amy had picked up her skirt in one hand, jumped off the boardwalk, and raced round the crowd in the opposite direction to Josh. Determined to catch this man, she hoped she could head him off and halt his escape from Josh. They had to know the truth. This cat-and-mouse game couldn't go on. Whatever Josh had done, surely it didn't merit all this hounding of him, intending to murder him. Whoever was behind the attacks, Amy felt, had no guts. If he had, he would come himself to face and kill Josh. She reached the crowd around the shrieking women and was passing behind it, but her intention was clear to the escaping stalker. What was he going to do? She wondered what his next move would be and felt the comforting heaviness of her gun in her pocket. Amy could see his eyes were wild, and they were darting around as he looked fruitlessly for an escape. What was he going to do?

CHAPTER FORTY-SIX

"I'll go to the right of the buggy crowd. You go to the left, Amy." Josh had said before he ran after the man. That was going to work when the crowd was stationary, but it would no longer be possible. The crowd around the buggy did not remain stationary. One woman jumped off the buggy and began screaming and shouting in a weird singsong. Her arms and legs were flung out in weird gestures as she danced around. The crowd moved back, still keen to watch her, but anxious not to let her get too close to them. Her hair broke free from its ribbons and streamed out in wild tendrils as she pranced around, calling upon the Devil as she did so.

"Oh, no!" Josh came to a stop as the people moved back and forth in front of him, blocking his route to the man he wished to speak to. His height enabled him to see over most of the crowd, and he caught sight of Amy with a frustrated expression on her face, which he thought must be like his own. He gave her a wave as he tried to push through the press of people. Amy waved back, and she, too, manoeuvred between the gawping crowd.

Breathless, Amy reached Josh's side, and they both looked round the crowd, unable to see their target. "Down there, he must have run down the alley between the saloon and hotel. We might still catch him yet," panted Amy, as she turned to run down the alley.

"Let me go first. He might be dangerous." Josh pushed past her, his gun ready in his hand. He reached the end of the alley first, and as Amy joined him, they both looked to either side of it. There were the backs of the saloon, the hotel, the sheriff's office, and a couple of private residences. Some were still being built: their timber still lying in piles. The tools of the workmen lay scattered about from when they'd been thrown down hurriedly as they'd run to see the goings-on in Main Street. Most buildings at the back were still made of tents, and it was going to be a fruitless task searching in every one of them.

"We lost him," Amy said, the disappointment in her voice apparent to Josh. He was also feeling frustrated at how the man had eluded them.

"If only we'd caught him, surely we could have got something out of him, couldn't we?" Josh said.

"If he's stalking you, Josh, he will be back. Next time, we'll be ready for him. I don't think he will find it so easy to escape us then," Amy said, laying her hand on his arm to sympathise with him.

"You're right, Amy, as usual, you always try to make the best of things. Yes, we'll be ready for him. Unfortunately, he knows that now, and he'll be ready for us looking out for him. If only that woman hadn't started that silly dance. What was wrong with her?" Josh said, his thoughts wandering back to the circumstances that had made the stalker's escape so easy.

"I don't know what was wrong with the woman. We can't do anything else here. He's gone for good. Let's get back and see what's happening with Mr Hobbs at the buggy." Amy gave a tug to Josh's sleeve, and he smiled down at her and nodded.

"Yes, Amy, I think my stalker is long gone now, hidden somewhere. We won't find him in this crowd, so we might as well go back and see what's happening. There's quite a noise coming from Main Street, and we don't want to miss it all."

They hurried back down the alley to see the crowd had

grown. Dora had appeared along with the sheriff, who was standing beside her with a look of horror on his face. Dora had her arms folded and an intent look which furrowed her brow as she watched the father. Mr Hobbs still sat on the buggy, a look of frightened resignation on his face as he looked from one daughter to the other.

"Any more like this at home?" Dora demanded. She walked up to the buggy, and she put one hand on the seat beside Mr Hobbs. "How long has this been going on for?"

Before Mr Hobbs could answer her, his other daughter, who'd been sitting on the buggy with her limbs twitching and jerking, suddenly leant forward and, with her finger outstretched, shrieked at Dora, "The Devil is in her! He lives with her. She's his whore!"

The shrieking words ended in a scream, and she flung herself off the buggy with her hands outstretched and launched herself at Dora. Her nails were like claws, and she sought to scratch the older woman's face. Manuel, who had been standing close by, rushed forward and grabbed one arm, and another burly man in the crowd grabbed her other one. She flung herself from side to side, shrieking all the while, and struggling with a superhuman strength. The men, who were twice her size, found it difficult to control her, but they fought against her, keeping a tight hold before she reached Dora. She gave a last shriek: "The Devil! She's in league with the Devil!" And she fell to the ground in a dead faint.

"What can I do? The others at home are sick and near death, and still more are shrieking and twitching and laughing wildly. I tell you, the Devil has come down from Devil's Mountain and taken over my entire household, and my brother's family as well. What can we do? And why am I the only one who is not sick or touched by the Devil? What can I do?"

CHAPTER FORTY-SEVEN

Mr Hobbs sank back on the seat of the buggy, put his head in his hands, and sobbed uncontrollably. The other daughter, who had been jerking with her arms and legs twitching around, looked back at her sister lying on the dirty Main Street and her father who still sat on the Hobbs family buggy sobbing. Then she looked round at the crowd. "The Devil has taken over our family. My father is unharmed." Here the girl pointed at her father. "He is unharmed because he is the Devil himself! My sister is now the Devil. And the Devil in her is dancing! The Devil is dancing in my sister." She screamed the words, her face twisted in a mixture of hatred and horror.

The crowd grew silent, and every eye was fixed on the father of the girls, Mr Hobbs, the older brother of the two who lived in seclusion out on their properties. The two girls had never even been seen in Nowhere, so it was difficult for the people to fully understand what they were seeing. Surely the girls didn't act like that all the time?

"Preacher, I've come for you, you must help. Surely you, as a man of God, can rid our family of their possession by the Devil? Look at my girls. Can you see how they are possessed? They are shy girls who can hardly speak to a stranger, but look at them now!" The crowd looked at them. Both girls were twitching and almost dancing in a raggedy, uncoordinated way. It was difficult to see how these two screeching girls could ever be quiet and shy.

The sheriff/Preacher stood watching the two girls before turning to look at their father. "I'm the sheriff now. I don't do much preaching work. Even if I was a full-time preacher, I wouldn't know how to get rid of the Devil from your family. It's a Catholic priest you need for an exorcism to get rid of the Devil. There's very few of them around here." He stood looking at the girls for a while. The tall, lanky figure of the man watched them intently, but after a few moments, he shook his long melancholy face. "I don't know, Mr Hobbs. This has got me beat."

Mr Hobbs stood up on the buggy and looked around at the crowd. He waved his hands at them and began earnestly pleading. "Can't someone help me? Some of them, especially the small children, are so sick; they lie in bed with the sickness and can't move, and then they cry out because they can see the Devil dancing. Surely someone can help me? I need someone to come out with me. My brother's family is the same. Please, can anyone help us?"

Meanwhile, Amy had walked back up to the general store and had joined Eliza, who was standing with her hands resting on the hitching rail, watching the scene enacted in front of her. Josh stood with Manuel, the two men as perplexed as the rest of the crowd.

"That's a terrible thing. The whole family struck down with the Devil working his evil way among them," Eliza said, and she shook her head.

"Have you seen anything like this before?" Amy asked the older woman. She too stood leaning against the hitching rail, her eyes fixed on the spectacle in front of them. "Even in the town where I lived before, we saw nothing like this."

"He's right, the father is right; there is a need for a priest here. The nearest one is in my hometown, and that is a two-day journey from here. That would take too long to help some of those poor children," murmured Eliza.

The sheriff was still standing, deep in thought. He

looked at the two girls and motioned the dancing one to come and stand beside her father at the buggy. Surprise at being beckoned by the tall, gaunt figure of the sheriff, who cut an imposing figure, she obeyed him. The sheriff was easily recognisable from one end of Main Street to the other, in his long black coat, black shirt, and baggy black trousers tucked into black boots. He stood in front of them and began intoning some prayers with his hands outstretched towards them. The indrawn breath of the watching crowd was audible as they watched, eagerly, wondering what would happen.

"That's the best I can do," the sheriff murmured to the father. "Don't know if that will do any good, though."

"No, he needs a priest. They would have a candle, holy water, and perhaps even the incense to shake over them. At least I think that's what they do, but they need a priest to rid them of the Devil and his evil ways." Eliza folded her arms and nodded her head wisely. She was a good Catholic, but with no church available, she had not gone to Mass regularly. Missing the sacraments was a worry to her, not to Manuel. He preferred to be away from the all-seeing eyes of the busybody priest who had presided over their small town.

Dora was already on the scene, with her customary rustling black clothes, and her constant chewing of tobacco. As a newcomer to Nowhere, Dora had taken a room in the hotel. It was soon realised that she was a helpful person to have around and could readily help where basic first aid was needed. She also provided care and advice to women in childbirth and had become valued by those women living their isolated lives around Nowhere. "Dora! You must help us," Mr Hobbs pleaded with her. Conflicted, the older woman stared at the two girls for a short time, then obviously thought for some moments before deciding.

That decision concerned Amy. The older woman stared at her for a long time, before calculating something in her head. Then her decision was made, she gave a nod to Mr Hobbs and said, "Change horses, and I'll be with you in a moment." Picking up her skirt in one hand, she negotiated the step up onto the boardwalk in front of the general store. She stomped along the wooden boards with an energetic determination that Amy felt was threatening. Somehow, she felt those heavy footsteps meant trouble for her. Dora's eyes rested on Amy before they looked Eliza up and down, finally lingering on that immense bulge beneath the tightly straining dress.

"Eliza, I think you are nearer to your time than you think. I wanted to be on hand to be with you and help you with the birth. But you can see how badly I am needed at the Hobbs' ranch. I'll only go to help them if Amy agrees to stay here with you." She leant over the rail and spat out the chew of tobacco, before wiping her mouth with a delicate lace handkerchief, edged in black.

Amy, despite the horrific words she was hearing, could not help but think about the contrast of the older woman chewing tobacco yet wiping her mouth with a delicate handkerchief. Then the words Dora had spoken seemed to rush into her mind. "What? I'm to stay here as company for Eliza until you get back. That's what you mean, isn't it?"

"Goodness, child, she does not need company. Eliza needs someone to help with the birth of her child. I want you to stay and help her when the child comes." Dora looked at Amy as if she was silly for not understanding what she meant.

A muffled snort of laughter from Josh behind her made Amy whirl around to face him. "If I'm staying to help, you can stay as well!" She'd moved so quickly that the braids that usually hung down took flight in a wild sweep behind her. "But, Dora, I won't know what to do. I've never seen a baby born. I don't..." Amy was pleading, almost begging. The fear that was overwhelming her, that the task the older woman was putting upon her, was so very frightening. That she, Amy Tanner, should assist in a childbirth was terrifying.

"You live out West in a frontier town. It's time you realised that, girl! Eliza has born a child before. She knows what to do, and she'll give you instructions. But she needs a woman with her as a support and help. Surely you can do that? You're not such a silly little girl as to run away from such a difficulty, are you?"

That snort of laughter came again from behind her. Amy was too terrified by the thought of coping with Eliza and a newborn baby to acknowledge it. And then she looked at Eliza. The Mexican woman was used to the realities of Western life, but now the plump woman's normally cheerful face was drawn into lines of worry. She looked at Dora with despair at the thought of losing the capable woman she had been relying on. That woman was leaving her alone with a young girl unused to the realities of life in the frontier environment.

Amy felt guilty. She was feeling upset and worried about helping Eliza with her birth. How awful it must be for Eliza to face that birth with no experienced woman at hand, only Amy herself. Amy clenched her fingers, feeling the heaviness of her Colt in her pocket. If only it was some bandit she had to shoot at, that would be much easier. But Eliza was her friend, and Eliza needed her.

"Yes, Dora, if someone could tell them at the Broken Horseshoe Ranch that Josh and I will stay here for a few days, we'll manage fine without you. I hope you can sort out the problems at the Hobbs' place. Don't worry about us here. We'll be fine, won't we, Eliza?" Amy pasted a bright smile on her face. She only hoped no one could see how false a smile it was!

CHAPTER FORTY-EIGHT

It was arranged, and a man from the livery stables was sent off to Broken Horseshoe Ranch with the message that Amy and Josh were needed at the general store and would stay overnight, possibly for a few days. Eliza was the first to turn away from Main Street and the crowd gathered there, going back into the store. Josh cast a last look at the retreating buggy before following Eliza. The two girls were still yelling and shouting, but now Dora was with them. Mr Hobbs was looking relieved, despite the peculiar behaviour of his daughters. Following on his usual black horse was the Preacher, because that was the role he was taking on when he was going out to the Hobbs' ranch. Unwilling to go, but aware of the overwhelming need for a man of religion to go, despite his claims he was of the wrong religion to cast out a devil, he had followed the Hobbs' buggy with his sheriff's element put on one side. Josh wondered how long Lance Grey, the man, could cope with his split duties as both sheriff and preacher. He foresaw difficulties ahead of the man.

The young lad riding off towards Broken Horseshoe Ranch was seen by Josh, and how he wished he could join the lad. What was he doing here? There was no way he could cope with the birth of a baby. He felt his stomach give a great lurch at the thought of a child being born and him having to help.

Josh realised his face must have gone green at this appalling thought because Manuel touched him on the arm, and after one look at his face, whispered in his ear, "Don't worry, we don't have to do much. I couldn't ask Dora to stay with us. The baby may not come for another few days. After all, at the Hobbs' place, people are ill. They may be dying. Dora is needed there. I'm sure we'll all manage if this little fellow comes sooner than expected." Manuel said this with a certain amount of false bravado, as he walked behind the counter and began straightening the already neatly labelled and sorted jars of jam. His nervous gestures showed he was not as confident as his words. Josh was still shocked at the thought of what he might have to do, and could only pray that this baby decided to come later, rather than earlier.

The next few hours were spent sorting out sleeping accommodations for Josh and Amy. A small storeroom had a mattress placed in it for Amy. This gave her privacy from the others and a reasonably comfortable bed to lie on. Josh, however, had to make do with the store itself. A corner behind the counter and out of the reach of the cooler night air coming in off the Main Street doors had a hastily stuffed sacking mattress of hay from the stable. Eliza found bedding and cushions, which she piled upon the makeshift mattress, with apologies for the haphazard nature of his bed.

"This is fine, Eliza. I think it's even better than the one I sleep on at the Broken Horseshoe Ranch," Josh said, sitting down on his new bed and bouncing up and down on the mattress.

"You are sure, Josh? I cannot make it any better?" The plump face of the Mexican woman, as she gazed down at the blonde-haired young man smiling up at her, lost its look of worry and fear. "Josh, you are so funny! I am so glad you are staying here. Both you and Amy make me feel so much better. Thank you both." As Josh stood up, smoothing down trousers that had a few wisps of hay clinging to them, he grinned at the woman, his eyes crinkling at the corners with the lopsided smile that he gave when he was truly content or happy. Eliza reached up and kissed him on the cheek, hugging him tightly. She then turned to Amy, pulling her close and kissing her soundly as well. She stepped back, gave them both another big beaming smile and, placing a hand to clutch the enormous bulge of her belly, she announced, "Food! We must eat, all of us must be well fed in case this one makes an entrance into the world and interrupts the meal!"

The meal had been one of laughter. Eliza and Manuel regaled the young couple with tales of life growing up in the Mexican village: the hardships they endured, but the laughter and love of family which overlay everything in such a close-knit community. The stories about the eccentric characters that entered and shopped in the general store brought forth laughter in disbelief of the baffling requests and antics of the customers. Amy, not to be outdone, had grown up in a small town in the East, and explained how the girl's school she attended had such petty rules and regulations concerning dress and deportment. To all their amazement, she described the rules of etiquette, how gloves and a hat were always to be worn, and the other essentials that made up everyday life in the community built around rigid strictures of the correct behaviour.

"How I love the freedom of dress that we have here. I love my boots." Here, Amy stuck out a foot, which was shod in a man's dusty, brown, square-toed boot. The meal ended, the dishes were washed, and the group went to bed, happy and content.

Amy was woken in the night by Manuel shaking her shoulder. "Amy, come quickly! Eliza says it's time."

Before she was properly awake, Amy saw Manuel's back as he ran out of the store cupboard where she was sleeping. Rubbing sleepy eyes and pulling her boots on, Amy rose from her makeshift bed and followed him into the main bedroom where he and Eliza slept.

"Eliza, what can I do?" were Amy's first words as she took in the sight of her friend seated on the bed, her feet firmly on the floor, the great bulk of her belly almost overflowing her knees. Her hair was plastered to her face, and she looked up at Amy with a white, worried expression.

"Oh, Amy, I think it's well on its way. When I had Ramon, it took hours and hours. It seemed to last forever. But I have been sitting here for some time and I swear this baby is coming quickly." She rubbed the swollen belly, then gasped at the pain of a contraction. "This baby will not wait for Dora's return. Amy! It's coming now!"

CHAPTER FORTY-NINE

The next few hours passed in a blur. Sometimes the minutes dragged interminably, and other times, they seemed to speed by. All Amy was conscious of was Eliza seated on the chair, gasping in pain at each contraction. Josh and Manuel had been banished from the room, and only when called upon did they supply drink, towels, and hot water.

Josh brought in yet another hot pot of tea. To everyone's astonishment, Eliza craved hot cups of tea. They seemed to give her strength, so the men began fighting over who could make the next pot of tea. Amy was delighted because she preferred tea, but so often there was only coffee to drink. Eliza stayed calm throughout the birth, despite her shouts and yells at the severity of the contractions. It was much to both women's relief that a baby girl arrived unexpectedly, and with little difficulty, considering the age of her mother. Instructed by the experienced Eliza on how to deal with the cord and the afterbirth, Amy managed everything with a calmness of manner that hid the emotional turmoil that was beneath her shaking hands and white face.

Wrapping the baby, after wiping her tiny body and face, Amy handed the child to her mother, and an overwhelming emotion surged within her. "She's beautiful, Eliza, and she has the most glorious brown hair. I'll get Manuel." Amy walked to the door, ready to call Manuel. She looked back at the mother and child on the bed and smiled at the joy, relief, and happiness that surrounded Eliza like a cloud.

Manuel rushed through to see his wife and the new child. Amy, walking into the general store properly for the first time since the baby started coming, looked around in dismay. Every shelf was empty of its goods. They were piled up on the counter and the floors, and Josh was standing with a cloth in one hand and a bemused look on his face.

"Manuel said it would take hours and hours. The best thing to do was to keep busy. He took everything down and we were going to clean the shelves thoroughly and wipe each provision before putting them back up. Now the baby has arrived..." Josh waved a hand around at the mess, then he realised what he had just said. "The baby, it's come? and Eliza? Are they both well? How did you manage, Amy? Come and sit down. You must be exhausted." He took some packets off a chair, put them on the floor alongside the others, and pushed it forward for Amy to sit.

"Yes, I'm exhausted, Josh. But it was such a wonderful miracle that I don't regret a minute. I've heard some horror stories of babies being born... well, never mind. Even Eliza said the last baby took hours and was far more painful than this little cherub. She is so beautiful, and it all went so well! If it hadn't, Josh..." Here, Amy gave a dramatic shudder, "I would never have managed. As it is, I'm..." Amy sank back against the chair, put her hands in her lap, and gave a deep sigh.

Josh went to the back of the counter, where there was a whiskey bottle already opened and two glasses standing beside it. Both had been well used. Taking another glass, he put a small drop in it, knowing Amy's dislike of alcohol, and gave it to her. "Drink it, Amy, you deserve it!" As he stepped forward and gave her the glass, his eyes fell upon her skirt and sleeves, and his eyes widened in horror as he caught sight of the bloodstains upon them.

"Sorry, Josh, I forgot I must look a mess. I cleaned up the baby and Eliza and their room, but forgot about myself." Amy took a large sip of the whiskey and coughed and spluttered, but she swallowed it. She rose to her feet, "I'll go and... But I've got nothing to change into." Amy sank back down in the chair, the exhaustion beginning to show on her face. She looked into the whiskey glass, swirled the liquid about, and then downed the lot.

"Whoa there, that's good whiskey. You shouldn't drink it like that," Josh said and added, "I don't mind you looking messy. I'm sure Eliza can lend you something to wear." He tried to keep his face straight, but it wasn't a success, and he had to burst out laughing. "Oh, Amy! If you could see your face at the thought of wearing one of Eliza's flouncy feminine dresses."

Amy glowered at him, and her tiny jaw jutted out. "There is no way I will dress in a flouncy outfit. I think Eliza said she had a new parcel of clothes come in yesterday. They haven't been unpacked, so perhaps we could see what's in it. Surely there would be something that would suit me better than a dress." She put the whiskey glass down on the counter with a decided thump. "Let's get this lot tidied away. If Eliza gets well enough to come out and see this mess, she won't be very happy." Amy rose to her feet, took the damp cloth from Josh, and began wiping the tins and jars of provisions, then handing them to him to place on the already cleaned shelves. As she worked, she became quiet and thoughtful.

"I wonder how Dora is getting on? Do you think the Devil has got into the Hobbs family? I don't think it's possible, do you? Could there be a Devil come to torment the people of Nowhere? "

CHAPTER FIFTY

By the time Manuel emerged, glowing with pride and delight at the birth of his baby daughter, Josh and Amy had finished cleaning the provisions and setting the whole general store to rights again. Eliza had baked that morning and, feeling the baby's stirrings within her, had put on an enormous pot of delicious chili which had been cooking gently throughout the day. They each enjoyed the food; the relief at the baby's safe arrival and Eliza's easy birth made the meal a joyous occasion. Manuel had taken Eliza's meal into her, unable to keep away from his beautiful new daughter.

Josh had been in to view the baby and had come out with a stunned expression on his face. "I thought babies were red and ugly when they were born. She is so beautiful, with that lovely brown hair." Manuel revelled in the compliments on his daughter, almost as if they were directed at him.

Despite Amy's protestations, both she and Josh were ordered back to Broken Horseshoe Ranch by Manuel and Eliza the next morning. The couple were ecstatic over the safe delivery of their baby and felt certain they could cope with the general store, as Manuel was not making any deliveries. They had Zach to call upon if Manuel needed extra help.

"Eliza wants to see you, Amy and Josh. Come into the bedroom. We have something to tell you. We have decided on a name for the baby," Manuel told them.

They followed him into the room. Eliza was seated with the baby, and she held her out for Amy to hold. Amy approached the bed nervously. The baby looked so tiny and fragile; she was frightened that she might drop her.

She sat on the edge of the bed beside Eliza and took the little one into her arms, holding her correctly as Eliza instructed. The tiny face was still wrinkled but looked beautiful when she was sleeping.

"You have been a great help to me, my dear. I know you were scared, but you stayed with me and helped me. To thank you, we're going to give this one my mother's name and yours. She will be Isabel Amy, so that she will always know and be grateful that you were with me," Eliza said.

Amy held the tiny little bundle in her arms, and an overwhelming love swept over her for the child. An overwhelming maternal love, which surprised her with its strength. Glancing up, she saw Manuel's beaming face alight with joy and happiness. Then her gaze wandered to Josh, and she saw an unusual expression on his face: one that she couldn't read at all. But she had no time to think about it, as her namesake decided she was hungry and cried. Amy enjoyed holding the baby whilst it slept but was uncertain of how she could cope with the tiny little thing crying so loudly!

"Thank you, Eliza; thank you, Manuel. I don't know what to say. I didn't know what to do, because I knew nothing about having a baby. All I could do was follow your instructions, Eliza. Are you certain you want to call the baby after me?"

She handed the baby back to Eliza, hurriedly now, as the cries were becoming louder and more urgent. Eliza took her child and smiled at the girl. "You'll never know how much you helped me just by being there. Amy, put your clothes and the other bloodstained materials out for washing. They will all be sorted out. Manuel will help me with the heavy lifting and washing, so you needn't worry about them. In that parcel which arrived yesterday, there is one of the new divided skirts in a blue heavy cotton fabric, which would be ideal for you to wear as you are on horseback so much. In the cupboard I have put a flannel blouse in the palest blue you can imagine. As soon as the pretty material came in, I immediately thought of you., Amy, I have been making it each evening for you as a birthday present. I think it is an ideal time to give it to you now, and it will be delightful with the blue skirt."

The excitement and gratitude flooded Amy's face as she found and looked at the beautiful garments Eliza had given to her. It took only seconds for her to whirl around and run into the storeroom she had used as a bedroom. The soiled garments she placed in the pile for Eliza, feeling guilty at leaving her friend with all that washing. But she knew that the big, burly, masculine Manuel was not above helping his wife in these sorts of tasks, and she knew he would help Eliza.

They left with Amy kissing her namesake and admiring yet again the beautiful little baby with the dark, curly hair.

CHAPTER FIFTY-ONE

Josh had said all the right things and smiled at the correct times, but he could not refrain from giving a tremendous sigh of relief as they drove out of Main Street. It had been a difficult time for Amy, he realised and understood that, but standing by and doing nothing whilst all the drama was being enacted in the other room had been difficult to bear. At least they could ride off into the sunny day with happy hearts, knowing they were leaving a contented family behind them. Josh wondered if he would ever become a father. It was something he'd never thought of before. Just fleetingly, it crossed his mind that he would love to see a girl baby wearing freckles across its tiny snub nose. He shook the thought out of his head and concentrated on the buggy and the track ahead of him. Beside him, Amy went quiet. As he looked down at her, he realised she was falling asleep, and putting his arm about her, he drew her close so that her head was upon his shoulder. Again, that thought crossed his mind. If he ever had a child, he would love it to look like Amy.

"Oh! That's the Broken Horseshoe Ranch sign. We're nearly home. I slept all that time, Josh? Why didn't you wake me?" Amy tidied her hair, which seldom needed doing as it always hung neatly down in her usual twin bunches or braids. Then she straightened her new blue skirt, stroking it lovingly. Amy pulled down the sleeves of her new blouse, smoothing the tiny creases out. Unexpectedly, Josh thought there was a decided feminine streak within her, which surprised him. Amy didn't like the fancy, frilly frocks that other women loved. Her style of clothing was practical, but she loved it to be new, or at least freshly washed.

It was with an overwhelming relief that Amy had seen the sign of Broken Horseshoe Ranch ahead of them. "Thank goodness we're home." Her voice held a note of surprise.

Josh looked at her, his eyebrow raised quizzically. "Why the surprise?" His deep voice held a trace of laughter. "It's where we've been riding to – Broken Horseshoe Ranch – for the last few weeks. So why so surprised?"

"Honestly, Josh, I'm surprised because I called this place home. Do you know, I never have felt it to be my home? Home in my mind was always the small house we had back East with..." Amy's voice broke and she took a deep breath. Josh had never heard Amy talk about her mother. None of the family ever did. He'd realised that early on when he'd come to live with them. It was because they felt her loss was so great that none of them could bear talking about her. "When the family was complete, all four of us, and before the influenza swept our neighbourhood, that house has always been in my mind as my home. We weren't the only ones to suffer in the epidemic. So many lost loved ones, and their families were broken up as one or the other parent died. We were so grateful that my father survived, sick as he was." Amy tossed her braids back over her shoulder, took off her hat, pushed it back and let it hang behind her, and gave him a shy smile. "But now, after all we've gone through and the trouble we've seen, this feels like home."

They rode in under the sign and Josh thought about Amy's remarks before turning to speak to her. "I don't remember anything else. Your ranch and your family are my entire world of knowledge. Did I grow up on a farm? Have I come from a city? My accent is, according to other people, either Eastern or even English. Which is it? So, Broken Horseshoe Ranch is my home until..."

Amy interrupted as Josh's voice faded away. "Until you regain your memory, then you may well discover that you have another home, with other people, that care for you." Amy finished the sentence Josh was struggling with. She knew that in all honesty to herself, she had to put that thought into the back of her mind. Josh came from another world to the desert ranch sitting in the foothills of the Devil's Mountain. That she had always known. When or if he discovered that other world, would he return to it without a backward glance to those who had helped care for him at Broken Horseshoe Ranch? He might never remember or give another thought to Amy Tanner.

Ben rushed up to them, Chan and Tom racing behind, eager to take their horses and also to get the latest news. Nancy and Luke were standing in the doorway, smiling at them.

"What's the news? What's happened?" Their voices seemed to merge into one as their eager questions showed their interest in the happenings of Nowhere.

Josh turned to Amy. "Go on, you tell them. It was all down to you helping Eliza."

Amy gave him a beaming smile and turned to the group eagerly awaiting the news. "It's a girl, and mother and baby are doing well. They are going to give the little girl her grandmother's name and mine! She's going to be called after me because I helped at the birth." Amy got down from the buggy and, when handing the reins to Ben, suddenly became aware of the silence.

"You helped deliver the baby? But what about Dora? Was there no other woman to help?" It was Nancy who spoke the words they were all thinking. How could little Amy possibly help deliver a child?

"There was no one at hand. Dora had to go out to the Hobbs' place with the Preacher. Amy was there and could stay with Eliza, and they didn't think the baby would come so soon. But Amy was wonderful. She helped Eliza, and the baby came quickly," Josh said. He didn't go into the details of how he and Manuel had walked up and down the stable yard, trying not to hear the cries and swear words from the normally quiet Eliza. It had been a tough time for Amy, but he felt he had fulfilled his part in the entire episode of the child's birth.

Both Amy and Josh sat back, tired after the strenuous time they'd had in Nowhere, and after their journey back to the ranch. Tom, they now realised, had in their absence taken over the entire kitchen, and all the cooking was done by him. Chan, meanwhile, revelled in the gardening. He and Nancy were expanding their plot each day, it seemed to Amy. But it was Ben who surprised her most, always he had his head stuck in a book or was scribbling. He'd write on anything, even the empty feed sacks or across the old newspapers. The words seemed to pour from him. But he had developed into a craftsman, turning his hand to making the commonplace items that were needed around a farm and home. Amy sat back in her chair and smiled at them all. "It's good to be home," she repeated.

Ben had moved away from the table and had reached for his pencil. His action jogged Amy's memory, and she rose to her feet, reached her cupboard bedroom, and grabbed her satchel. The well-worn canvas bag had done sterling duty over the years she'd had it, and it had become a familiar friend. She dived into it, pushing aside

the essentials that were needed for a girl living in a
frontier country. "Here it is! This came in the mail. It's
a letter to you, Ben." She came forward and handed it to
her brother.

CHAPTER FIFTY-TWO

"For me? A letter for me?" Ben studied the letter, turning it over, staring at the back, even stroking it. He held it to the light of the oil lamp that was set upon the table as if to see what was in it without even opening it.

"Open it, Ben!" His father's words made him jump, and he reached forward to pick up a knife that was lying on the table after the meal. Checking that the knife was clean and had not been used, Ben inserted it with a shaking hand, slipped it under, and opened the envelope. He pulled out a folded sheet of paper, and as he opened it, two coins fell out onto the table. "It's money. There's money in the envelope." Ben stared down at them. He stretched out his hand and, with his finger, touched the pair of coins lying on the table where they had landed.

"Read the letter, Ben." Luke's voice held an increasing note of impatience. They were all eager to find out what this letter, and the unexpected money, meant. Who had sent money to Ben? Why had they sent money to Ben? They watched him in eager anticipation as he slowly read the letter.

Ben gave a gulp. His eyes seemed to fill with tears, and he swallowed hard. Wordlessly, he handed the letter to his father.

Luke held the letter closer to the light of the oil lamp. He read it through slowly, looked at his son, and read it again. He placed it on the table and contemplated it. "You have earned money from your writing, Ben. This is something I didn't foresee. I never imagined your scribbles would ever amount to much. Ben, I am sorry. I was mistaken, and you have proved that. They say they loved your account of our move out here to the desert country. Not only are they going to publish it and send you money, but what is most rewarding is that your writing has now been proven to be a worthwhile occupation." Luke reached forward and took a swallow of his coffee. He took another deep breath before continuing. "Best of all news, they wish you to continue narrating the stories of how life is lived on Broken Horseshoe Ranch in the foothills of the Devil's Mountain."

The noise was tremendous. Everyone spoke at once. Amy even went out of the cabin to shout for Leah, Ezra, and the veteran, Bill, who had taken up residence with them in their cabin. They rushed in, and everyone patted Ben on the back and congratulated him so much that he was almost overcome with emotion.

"Read it to us, Ben! You must read it out to us. We want to know what was said in your article." Josh was the first to suggest this, but the others soon followed suit, and Ben went over to his quilt bedding and produced the dog-eared notebook.

Ben read from his notebook, hesitantly at first, looking up for approval as he managed the first couple of sentences. His audience was listening eagerly and with astonishment. Over the years, they had all watched as Ben scribbled away. Not one of them had ever bothered to ask to read any of his writing, or even suggest he read it out loud to them. Ben had written about the journey – from that initial packing up, through the difficulty in deciding what was necessary to embark on a new life out West. The actual journey itself had been portrayed with amusing candour, neither minimising the hardship nor exaggerating it. When he'd finished the short piece of writing, they could understand how it was acceptable to an Eastern audience.

"No wonder this writing sold. It is excellent, Ben," was Josh's remark. It was the first comment, but not the last. Everyone congratulated Ben again on his achievement. The boy looked at the two coins he had earned through his writing, the very first acknowledgement of his talent. He pushed them towards his father. "That's the first money. They want me to write a weekly article to put in the magazine. They will pay me for each one."

Amy's chair hurtled backwards as she jumped up and flung her arms around her brother. "Well done, Ben! I am so proud of you."

Ben was embarrassed but delighted. That evening was remembered by all at Broken Horseshoe Ranch as the happiest they had ever had. It was remembered most of all by Ben, who went to sleep clutching his notebook. His eyes strayed continually to the two coins still sitting on the table, each time he woke in the night with a smile on his face.

CHAPTER FIFTY-THREE

That morning, Josh and Amy set off for Lonesome Creek early, whilst it was still dark. This longed-for expedition had been planned to follow the new clues Luke and Ezra had identified. Luke was certain these would lead Josh and Amy to the Jesuit gold. Dawn was a faint golden glow on the horizon, behind the jagged peaks of the Devil's Mountain. "So much has happened that it seems ages since we've been out searching for the Jesuit gold. Nowhere has relatively few buildings and even fewer people, but I find it oppressive now. I've got used to the open spaces: the horizon stretching away in the distance; the impressive sight of the huge towering peaks behind us; and always that vast expanse of sky," Josh said, as they rode along. His words were more to himself than Amy. The realisation hit him of how much he loved this wild country that he now lived in.

Amy was silent. She thought hard about these words that came from Josh. It was unusual for him to express his feelings in such a frank manner. On the surface, Josh seemed open and good-natured, which he was (Amy admitted to herself), but it only went so far. Being so much in his company, perhaps she was the only one who realised the depth to which he hid his true feelings and thoughts. She caught him looking at her, awaiting a reply to his words.

"I was thinking about what you're saying. When I first came here, I longed for streets and bright lights, the shops and houses, and the bustle in the morning as people went to work. Shopping was a spur-of-the-moment thing, whereas here it takes a journey to get to the general store, and even when you get there, they may not have what you're looking for. I don't know when it happened, but like you, my longing for civilisation gradually left me." Amy threw out her arm, encompassing the scenery as they rode on. "Each morning the dawn sky is so beautiful, the mountains have dark colours of midnight-blue and purple, but when the sun hits the rocks, they glow with orange and red. The sentinel cacti have become familiar to me. I love them; the way they march up the hillsides. The land that used to be dry-baked and frightening at midday is now just an everyday occurrence. Riding along the creekside, listening to the gurgle of water over the rocks and boulders, is so different from the clattering carriages and horses and the noisy, smelly street vendors that we found when we were living in towns."

They both turned to each other and smiled. There was no more to be said. Both agreed that this land, unforgiving and demanding of those who tried to settle on it, had got under their skins, and they loved it deeply. Somehow, the nature of the land and its difficulties made them appreciate the small victories they had in establishing a life for themselves.

Excitement grew within them when they reached the familiar search area. The boulder with the distinctive hole within it now towered on top of a rocky cliff above them. They were deep in the canyon of Lonesome Creek. Tethering the horses to some trees that grew beside the river, both sat down on a fallen log to eat their lunch and look again at the map. There were no other instructions on the map. Luke had spent many hours trying hard to decipher the secrets of the map, and he had determined that a cave was where they had to go next. They couldn't see a cave beneath that boulder, or on either side of it, as they gingerly walked across and around the enormous boulders that lay scattered at the foot of it. Tired, they returned to the log to sit and look again at the map.

Amy sat on the log drinking from her water bottle, which she had filled from the fast-flowing creek beside them. Josh had lifted the map and was standing beside her, looking again and again at that cliff face. "We must be missing something. There must be some way of finding that cave. What if we..." Josh never finished that sentence.

The gunshot rang out loud in the canyon's silence, which had been previously only broken by the gurgling of the river. Josh fell to the ground and reached up to pull Amy down behind the log beside him. He needn't have bothered. Amy had fallen flat beside him in the second after the gunshot echoed around the canyon.

"Who's shooting at us?" Josh gasped, and he clutched his arm where the blood was welling up and trickling through his fingers.

Amy, beside him, gave his wound a cursory glance and, realising it wasn't serious, looked away, searching for the gunman. "I don't know, but his shots are coming from beneath the cliff face behind those boulders." She edged towards the end of the log and peered around it. "We were sitting ducks where we were. I expected no one else to be here. A stupid mistake I will never make again," Amy said. Taking her gun out of her pocket, she checked it and readied it for action. "Can you still shoot, Josh? Is your wound so bad you can't use your gun?"

CHAPTER FIFTY-FOUR

Josh grimaced as he tried to hold his gun, but he managed it and gave Amy a determined nod and a weak smile. "I can shoot."

"Throw out the map, and I'll let you live. No one but me is going to get that Confederate gold." The harsh voice came from the rocks and boulders. Another shot was fired in their direction.

Josh stared at Amy as they both moved further down behind the log. "Confederate gold? What's he talking about?" Josh muttered to Amy.

Amy crawled further along behind the log and peered round it, looking towards the area where the voice had come from. She saw a man wearing a tattered Confederate uniform and holding a rifle, which he aimed towards the log. Fortunately, he was looking in Josh's direction and was unaware of her scrutiny of him.

"Tell him we're not after Confederate gold, we're looking for the lost gold of the Jesuits," whispered Amy, as she moved back to join Josh.

"We don't want your Confederate gold. Our map shows where the Spanish Jesuits went, and where they buried their gold. We know nothing about Confederate gold. We're going after Jesuit gold." Josh's voice echoed in the narrow canyon as he shouted across to the man.

Amy crawled back again to the lookout hole she had discovered in the log. She saw the man thinking about this before he slowly lowered his rifle. "He's putting down his rifle," she whispered to Josh.

"Where did you get your map from?" The harsh voice asked.

"A Mexican guy on his deathbed gave it to my friend

along with our Spanish gold coin. It led us to the boulder up the hill that has a hole in it," was Josh's reply.

"I'll put my gun down and come over and look at your map. Mine shows Confederate symbols only. If yours has the same symbols, I'll know if you're lying to me."

Amy, watching the man, saw him place his gun on the ground and walk towards them. She stood up slowly. But she had her hand in her pocket, her Colt at the ready if he should shoot at them again. Josh had his arm held across his chest as it bled out. He clutched it with his good arm as he, too, stood up and walked towards the man. The map was folded and under his arm. He gave a sideways glance towards Amy and gave a slight smile as he saw that hand of hers in her pocket. Josh knew she would not want to pull the trigger. One skirt was already bloodstained, with a hole in the pocket where she had shot the man that threatened both her and Eliza in the general store. He remembered how distressed she had been at the damage to her skirt. She was wearing her new one today, and he hoped she didn't have to shoot the man. Not because of the man's death. No, that wasn't his major worry. It was because Amy would be good and mad if she had to shoot a hole in her new skirt!

"As you can see, I'm from the Confederate Army." The weary blue eyes travelled over both of them. To Josh's amusement, he dismissed Amy, not realising how lethal the girl could be. But his eyes narrowed as he searched Josh for any clue to his background and identity. When none was forthcoming, he asked outright. "Who did you fight for? What side were you on?"

"I don't know," was Josh's immediate reply. "Because of a head injury, I lost my memory. I don't know which side I fought on." What Josh didn't tell the man was the certainty that he fought on neither side. How or why he thought that, he couldn't have said. But within himself, he knew he took no part in the American Civil War.

The man looked at Amy for confirmation of Josh's remarks. "It's true. I found him unconscious and with a head injury. He had been left for dead, with no identification on him. He remembers nothing."

"Let's see your map then," the man said, and sat down beside them on the log. First, he whistled, and a burro trotted out from beside the rocks to join them. The man reached up and grabbed a bottle, from which he took a swig before offering it to the others. They refused. He shrugged his shoulders and then looked at the map which Josh gave to him.

Josh didn't enjoy handing over their precious map, but so much of what was on it only showed the landmarks. The actual signs that the Jesuits had made, and what they were looking for, were within their minds and not written on the map. On previous searches, they had found those Jesuit signs and followed them, so they now knew what to look for. Knowing those signs were not on the map made Josh feel easier when he saw the map in the stranger's hands.

Examining the marks intently, the man repeatedly scrutinized their map. Josh watched as he seemed to acknowledge the differences between both maps. He had his folded map in his hands, but he didn't offer it to either of them, keeping it well away from their gaze. The well-worn uniform he wore had tattered trouser ends, and he had a heavy cotton dust jacket over the top of the greasy uniform. His age could have been anything between twenty and forty. The lines etched deep on his face bore witness to the hardship he had suffered whilst on active service and afterwards. Both Ezra and Ben had regaled Josh with the history of the Civil War and the disastrous damage it had wrought on the States of America. Especially, they told him about the after-effects on the southern states. Amy stood a little way off, alert and at the ready, one hand in her pocket on her gun, and Josh knew the other hand was ready to reach behind her back for the knife she kept hidden. She didn't trust this man, nor did he.

"Yes, you're looking for something different from me. I'm going to the end of this canyon, and then I go on further into the foothills, following the signs of the Knights of the Golden Circle. They took the gold from Richmond, and it's hidden in secret caches throughout the States. I heard tell of one. It will only take a couple of days to ride from here, so I'll be on my way." He rose from the log and handed the map back to Josh before casting envious eyes on their horses. Then he reached for his burro and set off without a backward glance. He stooped to pick up the rifle he had dropped on the ground on the way.

Amy took a hand out of her pocket, walked over to Bella, and took the rifle from its scabbard. She made sure it was loaded and placed it beside her on the log. She sat back down again. "I don't trust him. He was looking at our horses and our gear. I think we should leave now, after I have washed your wound and bound it up, ready for your journey home."

Luckily, the bullet had only grazed Josh's arm, and the bleeding had soon stopped. All the time they were conscious of being on the alert, fearful of the man's return. They had spent a couple of hours looking around the area and would have perhaps spent another hour searching. Not now, not after their encounter with the strange man. They didn't trust him and felt it was best to get away from his vicinity.

Josh stood guard with the rifle, while Amy packed up her things and mounted Bella. She sat on her horse facing the direction the man had been going, her eyes constantly on the lookout for any sightings of him. Her rifle was poised, ready to fire. In no time at all, Josh was mounted on Star, and they turned and set off for home. They moved quickly, eager to get away from the man.

CHAPTER FIFTY-FIVE

That night, the meal was interrupted by David. The baby was always restless when they were eating. It had become a routine with him. "I'll take him out on the porch and walk up and down with him whilst Josh tells you about today's search," Amy said. She held the baby David in her arms and went out into the cooling air. He nestled into her arms and seemed to quieten when she walked up and down, humming to him. His blonde curls tickled her nose, and those fingers appeared, always searching for her braid. He grabbed it and thrust it into his mouth, trying to chew on the hair and ribbon at the end.

"No, you don't," Amy laughed at the baby and threw her braid back over her shoulder. He was silent for a moment and stared at her as if realising that she had deprived him of his favourite chew thing on her person. But Amy pulled from her pocket the tiny little rag doll that had come with him. Chubby fingers closed around it and he gave a gurgle as if recognising an old friend. One leg, and one leg only, was thrust into his mouth, and he chewed on it. "Only that leg will do? You don't chew the other bits of it, do you?" David paused in his chewing, to stare up at her as if thinking about her remark, then chewed a few times more before snuggling into her shoulder. He fell asleep.

David had arrived with his Indian blanket and swaddling close around him. There had been a distinctive aroma to him, not unpleasant, of herbs, fresh air, and some kind of oil that had been smoothed on the baby's skin. Amy had inhaled the scent of baby David when he had arrived. Sadly, that aroma had left the child. Now he smelt of Tom's cooking and Nancy's well-washed clothes and her homemade soap with her favourite herbs within it. David, with his blonde hair and now his clothes and his fresh smell of the Broken Horseshoe Ranch, was no longer an Indian baby. He was fast becoming one of them. Apart from his darker skin than the average white baby, Amy thought she couldn't see any Indian heritage remaining in him.

Amy sat down on the bench. The door into the cabin was open a crack, and she could hear the conversation while she sat nursing David. "We didn't trust the man at all. I think he would like to have taken our horses from us and all our gear. But he could see we were armed and wary of him. When he went one way, we loaded up and returned as quickly as we could to the ranch."

"There are so many rootless ex-soldiers from both sides, North and South, that are roaming around seeking a purpose in life," Luke sighed.

"Seeking an easy way to steal stuff, if you ask me. Our Bill and Nat found good homes and are now working for a living despite their crippling injuries. Wandering around looking for hidden gold is one thing. Hoping to steal goods and horses from people is quite another," Nancy said, shaking her head in disgust.

"I've heard about the Confederate gold," said Ben. "It was in a magazine I read before we moved here. There was a train carrying money from the Confederate Treasury and it vanished. I think it was in Richmond. Some banks were robbed and payroll stolen; all to go into a fund to help the Confederate Army rise again. All this gold was split up and hidden away in secret places, ready for an uprising. This article said people stand watch over these places and are keeping it hidden for... I don't know for what," Ben finished lamely.

"That's a lot of information, young Ben," said Nancy, looking at the boy. "Why are you so interested in that?"

"Pa was looking for the Jesuit gold. I thought we might keep a lookout for any signs of the Confederate gold at the same time." He gave a grin and looked around at them all. "Just fancy if we found both sets of gold!" Laughter rang around the cabin, and it was with cheerful smiles on everybody's faces that they finished the meal. Unfortunately, their uproarious laughter woke David!

CHAPTER FIFTY-SIX

Josh and Amy set off for Nowhere the next morning in a happy state of mind. They had left the happy family at the general store with their new arrival of Isabel Amy. Both were looking forward to seeing the baby, because even after a few days, she may have grown or changed in some way. That's what Amy was thinking anyway.

"I'm so pleased that Ben had the encouraging letter and payment for his writing. With Bill now helping him with grammar and spelling, he may well have a career in journalism," Amy said, as they drove on the track to Nowhere.

"Maybe your father won't pester him to go back to school or college back East. Ben has taken to the outdoor life here. I don't think he'd survive in a city now. Honestly, Amy, I'm uncertain of where I lived before, but I would find it hard to live anywhere but here." Josh flung out an arm as if to illustrate how he was feeling about the surrounding countryside.

Behind them, the homestead with its flourishing, neat gardens, the small number of animals they kept, and the two ramshackle barns were overshadowed by the Devil's Mountain looming over the foothills and ranch beneath. Dawn was breaking, and the sun's rays hit the soaring peaks with their sheer cliff faces, illuminating them into fiery oranges and reds. The rocks and boulders almost came alive under the harsh glare of the morning sun. Dark crevices and caves became more mysterious as their shadows grew darker against the illuminated landscape surrounding them. No longer black, now the tints and hues of purple and midnight blue created a depth that was both intriguing and frightening, promising hidden treasure or frightening chasms and caverns.

"For me, it's the freedom I love," said Amy. She thought for a while before adding, "My life is no longer governed by the rules and traditions of a small town. I can't imagine myself going back to school, even as a teacher, which is what Pa wanted me to do. Working in an accepted job or profession back East, I couldn't wear my favourite hat, my suede jacket with the fringes, a skirt with pockets to hold a gun and knife, and my comfortable men's boots!" Her laughter rang out as they neared Nowhere.

They were both smiling with the contentment that came from like-minded companions, after a pleasant journey and enjoyable conversation. But as they drew into the small township, they became aware of shouting and screaming in the centre of Main Street.

"It's happened again! The Devil has taken a life this time." Slim ran up to them. He put a hand on Bella's reins, causing her to stop. He was so eager to tell the story to the newcomers. His face was a mask of excitement and glee at the terrible tidings he had to impart to them. "It's old man Thompson. The Devil killed him last night. They found him, and it could only have been the Devil that had done him to death, all mutilated and cut as he was." Slim looked behind them. He saw another rider coming into town. Ignoring their cries of horror and Josh's questions, Slim ran off to impart his horrific tidings to another new pair of ears.

Bella began moving towards the stable yard behind the general store as usual. Stunned as they were, Bella was allowed to carry on, despite their interest in the crowd gathered outside the sheriff's office. As they turned into the yard, they passed the boardwalk of the general store and could see Manuel standing there talking to another rancher.

"Manuel will know what's happening. We'll get Bella settled and then find out the actual truth, not Slim's garbled version of whatever's happened," Josh said, as he jumped down from the buggy.

"This is dreadful, that poor old man. He came to this land with such high hopes; I can't believe he died in such a terrible way. The property he bought was no good, had no water, he could barely survive. He was trying to sell it to move away. Why did this have to happen to him now?" Amy said, as she lifted out her bag and put it over her shoulder. Bella, happy and content, was left as they both walked slowly up the steps and into the back of the general store. Neither wanted to go in and find out what was happening. Another horrific occurrence was not to be rushed towards.

"We had a lovely night. It was such fun and even Pa looked well and happy. The journey into Nowhere was pleasant. The morning sun was not too hot, and we had a..." Amy's voice faded away and she looked at Josh.

"Yes, it seems terrible on such a morning that there should be such a horrible beginning to our day," Josh said. He knew the words were simple because he found it difficult to put his thoughts on this fresh tragedy into words that could explain the horror and disgust he felt. No actual devil was wandering around the mountains. No, some man had evil in his heart; so much so, he became a very devil himself!

CHAPTER FIFTY-SEVEN

"Isabel is lovely. She's sleeping peacefully, and Eliza says that she has been a good baby. She sleeps most of the time and gurgles happily when she is awake. Eliza was going to get up, but I told her to stay in bed longer now we had arrived. We had an early start, and it won't take long to get the general store clean and tidy after yesterday. I know Eliza used to do it each night, and she was so apologetic about missing last night. So silly, as if I don't know she's got a new baby to look after, and it's just after she gave birth!" Amy wrapped Eliza's huge white apron around her waist. The ties went round her slim figure twice. In seconds she had swung into action, brushing the floor clean of the dust that the previous day's customers had trodden onto the wooden floor. Going outside, Josh saw her give a glance up to the crowd still outside the sheriff's office before turning her back on it and energetically sweeping the entire boardwalk clear of dust and debris.

While Amy was busy with the broom, Josh had unloaded vegetables from Nancy and Chan's vegetable garden. There had been a surplus again, and they both had been delighted to hand over to Josh baskets for him to take to Manuel.

"Manuel, Nancy sent these vegetables for you to sell. Will they be of use to you?" Josh stood looking down at the produce before looking up at Manuel as he strode back into the store.

Manuel walked over, looked down, and fingered a few of the items from each box. He smiled at Josh. "These are of excellent quality. Tell Nancy I can always sell produce of this quality. How does she want to be paid? Do I give her money for them? Or goods? Most of my customers prefer goods in exchange. Do you know, Josh? Some days, very little cash exchanges hands in this store. Some people have accounts, I do set a limit on credit, but I have to! But often it's goods we exchange, or even tasks. Seth in the saloon pays me in beer and whiskey and gets provisions in exchange. Mind you, Josh, I'm finding it hard to keep track of my account book. Are you or Amy any good at figures?" Manuel said as he produced a dogeared notebook, with pieces of paper falling out of it. "It's all got a bit of a muddle," he added before putting the account book on the counter and shoving a few pieces of paper back in after they fell out.

"I don't know if I can do that sort of paperwork. Can you do it, Amy?" Josh said and turned to the girl as she came back in with the broom.

"I'm not sure. They did mathematics at my school. If you want, Manuel, I can always look at your book. Have you another new one? That one looks a bit of a mess," Amy said, squinting at the notebook and its mess of papers on the counter.

Josh had never seen Manuel move so fast. The store owner dashed across the store to a drawer set in a large wooden cupboard and produced another notebook, and a smart new book labelled cash. Scrabbling about in the drawer, he then produced with a flourish a large box containing pencils, ink, and pens. "This was here when Eliza and I bought the store from the former owner. He had started it with such high hopes, but his wife lasted only six months living in Nowhere. She told him, in no uncertain terms, she would leave whether or not he went with her. This is what he used to keep all his daily cash bills in." These were thrust into Amy's hands. Startled at this bundle pushed towards her, Amy dropped the broom and grabbed the stuff Manuel was putting into her hands.

"Manuel, I only did mathematics at school. I'm not sure if I'm able to do this properly," Amy protested, as she looked down at the box and the books in her arms.

Manuel beamed at her. The chubby-faced man seemed to believe that she would manage fine. There was a small table at the back of the store, which was used to organise the parcels and mail that came in. The solitary parcel awaiting the carrier from the town of Duloe was placed on a shelf. Manuel turned back to Amy, took the parcel of new books and box of pens and pencils from her, and placed the lot on the recently cleared table. He then dashed back to the counter, where he grabbed the messy cashbook and its multitude of scribbled notes. "There you are, Amy, you can get started on those right away. I'm not doing any deliveries today. Tomorrow, Josh and I will do deliveries because Zach has promised to spend the entire day here with you. Josh and I will look after the store, while you get started on the accounts."

Josh snorted with laughter. He couldn't help himself. Amy's face was a picture. She was looking horrified at the small table littered with pieces of paper and all the bits and bobs that Manuel had dredged out of that drawer. He swallowed his grin. He knew it wasn't fair on Amy to laugh at her. Josh only hoped that her mathematics lessons at school had been good ones!

Startled by the opening of the front door of the shop, they all turned to see the sheriff walk in. His normally melancholy face was now even longer and more miserable if that had been possible. "Good morning, I need coffee and plenty of it," he said and put the coins down on the counter. "Don't ask me about it. I will tell you this, old man Thompson died and then the mark of Satan was put on his body. There were devil markings all around the property, and I found another chicken treated in the same manner as the one found on Main Street. It's a dirty business. That poor man never had a good day's luck since he set foot on the property."

"What will happen to it now? Did he have any heirs?" Manuel asked.

Taking his coffee, the sheriff stared at him as if thinking hard about whether to tell them his thoughts. As if deciding, the sheriff put his coffee bag back down on the counter. "It's a strange thing, but I didn't think old man Thompson could write very well. I know for a fact that he had no family to leave the property to. That's why he was so eager to sell it. What should I find laid out on top of a dresser, all handy like, was his last will? Supposedly written by him and written well and in a fine language." The sheriff paused, his eyes moved from one of them to the other. He watched for their expressions as if he gauged what they were thinking.

Josh realised their expressions must have been satisfactory because the sheriff nodded his head in satisfaction. "Yes, you have all thought the same as me. Decidedly peculiar, that's all I'm saying. That will, written out like that, was decidedly peculiar." He picked up his coffee and gave them a nod. "Thanks. I'll get back to the office and brew a fresh pot." And he marched towards the door.

"Wait! Sheriff, wait. You haven't told us. Whose name was written in the will? Who did old man Thompson leave his property to?"

CHAPTER FIFTY-EIGHT

Sheriff Lance Grey paused at the doorway. His tall figure stood still for a long moment as if he was wondering whether he should tell them the truth. He shrugged his muscular shoulders, the long black coat he wore swinging from side to side, and he turned to the group. "Might as well tell you now. You'll know soon enough. He left the property to that new fellow staying at the hotel, Charles Roberts." The door closed behind him before the outbreak of exclamations could be heard.

"Why did old man Thompson leave the property to him? He wouldn't sell to him, so why leave it to him?" Amy said.

"Something is not right about this. No, this isn't right at all. The sheriff thinks there is something wrong, you can tell by his attitude." Manuel watched the sheriff go down the street, clutching his bag of coffee and nodding to the few people about. "No, I don't think our sheriff is too happy about this."

"There's no proof of any wrongdoing. Roberts will inherit the land, and there's nothing anyone can do about it. That man can sell the plots to the unsuspecting buyers legitimately now. It's his land to do what he likes with," Josh said, his face set and hard. He didn't like Charles Roberts at all. He had disliked the man since he arrived in town. But he hadn't reckoned on how evil the man was behind that smarmy exterior and that false smile of his. While he was talking, he was watching Amy. Even meeting her for the first time, Charles Roberts had made his feelings for the girl plain. He had liked her. A lot. Amy had at first been flattered by his attentions, but now she actively disliked him. Josh was pleased about that.

"I wonder if the problems around that property with the markings and banshee sounds of the Devil will stop now?" Amy said thoughtfully, straightening the books that she had been given by Manuel to do the accounts on the table. "Can anyone prove it was him? Or will he just get away with it?"

"There's nothing we can do. Nothing." Manuel said. "I'm going to tell Eliza about this." He left them both, still shaking his head at the latest turn of events.

"Can you sort out those books?" Josh said, as he walked over to look down at the mess of papers and books on the table. As Amy opened the book Manuel was using for his accounts, even more papers and notes spilt onto the table. Amy was horrified at this additional mess added to her task. "I'd offer to help you, but one thing I am certain of, despite losing my memory, I am no good with figures. Don't ask me how, I just know that."

The brand-new account book was pulled from the pile of notes. Amy smoothed down the cover and opened the pristine pages within it. "I can't do any worse than this," she gestured to the mess on the table. "If all I do is write these notes out neatly, in date order in the account book, surely that will be better than what we have now."

"Anything would look better than that muddle," Josh said and began sorting out the vegetables that he had brought from Nancy's garden from Broken Horseshoe Ranch. "Did Nancy give you a list of all the goods and provisions she wants in exchange for these?"

"Yes, yes," Was Amy's mumbled reply as she bent over her mountainous pile of papers on the table.

Josh watched her and smiled to himself. Amy was concentrating hard. Her face was solemn and, whenever she was fully absorbed, Josh knew that the tip of her tongue poked out from between her lips. He watched for it, and sure enough, it appeared, making her look like a six-year-old child.

The basket was arranged just as Manuel liked, and it was ready to go out on the boardwalk, with the other fresh vegetables and eggs that were always displayed to tempt the customers inside. Josh picked it up, then almost dropped it as he saw who was about to enter the store. Standing at the back of the store, Josh was in shadow, and anyone coming up to the door would not have seen him. Josh recognised the man at once. He was the one who was watching him and following him. "Amy! Look who's coming into the store. Go and serve him, whilst I hide from him. When he gets inside, I'll get up and grab him. Then we'll find out what he's doing here and who sent him. "

CHAPTER FIFTY-NINE

Josh flung himself down behind some barrels of pickles. He screwed up his nose at the aroma that came from the pungent pickles, so beloved by many of the cowboys and ranchers.

"Can I help you?" Amy said, as the figure approached the counter uncertainly. He stared at her, wondering if she was the one that had chased him the day before. The polite question from Amy allayed his fears, and he stepped forward and asked her for several provisions. Reaching up to the shelves behind her, Amy put several of the items on the counter. A glance towards Josh, and she continued serving the man. Puzzled, Amy wondered why Josh hadn't acted but continued serving the man. Placing a packet of beans on the counter, followed by the two cans of condensed milk, she began questioning him. "Is this your first time to Nowhere? Are you planning to stay here long?"

The man began putting his provisions into a large canvas sack. He didn't look up at her while he was doing this. Finding the silence after her questions too uncomfortable, he looked up at her finally and answered. "No, just passing through, getting provisions ready to travel on up country. Don't plan on staying here at all."

Amy counted up the cost of his provisions and told him the total. All the while, she was staring at his face. Josh had been right. The man had a birthmark across his face. It was partly obscured by the enormous whiskers, moustache, and beard he wore. Amy was certain they were false. His face seemed to move when he spoke, but his whiskers didn't. Taking a closer look, she felt certain she saw clumps of glue at the side of one whisker. "Have you business here in Nowhere?" Amy said and looked towards Josh.

"Yes, your business here in Nowhere? Have you perhaps come to kill me?" Josh moved silently behind the man, standing between him and his escape through the door. "I want to know who sent you to kill me. And I want to know why he wants me dead!" The voice of Josh was soft but laced with an intent to get the answer by any means from the man. The man had whirled around to stare at Josh. He visibly paled and edged back towards the counter. A glance behind him and he went even whiter, if that was possible, when he saw Amy standing with her gun pointed straight at him.

"Let me go, let me take my stuff and go. Here is the payment for my provisions. Just let me go. I was leaving Nowhere anyway. I shouldn't have taken the job, but it seemed like good money, and I was broke. You see, I'm not used to this sort of thing." The man's voice wavered with fear, and the whiskers seemed to have a life of their own as they went up and down with his nervous shakes.

"Answer my questions, and you can go." Josh moved closer to the man, the gun still pointing at the man's heart. "Now!"

Amy readied her gun behind the man, and the loud click made him jump and turn round to stare at her nervously. "I think you'd better do as the man says. Answer the question, or you won't be going anywhere." The gun was held steady in her firm little hand, but there was no hesitation in her face. The man, seeing the resolution in her eyes and turning back to see the even sterner expression on Josh's face, seemed to wilt before them.

"I was talking to a man in a bar and saying how I was looking for work. A smartly dressed man came up behind me and offered me a large sum of money if I would kill the man known as Josh Barnes in Nowhere. He didn't give me a reason, and I didn't ask. I was so broke that I felt able to do the job. Heavens, so many men died during the war, what's one more? That's what I thought until I came to Nowhere. Then I saw you, and somehow you weren't an anonymous person to be gunned down and walked away from. When you saw me and chased me, I hid in a tent building, and decided I would leave town." In a sudden movement, he tore off the false beard, whiskers, and moustache and threw them on the counter. "Ridiculous idea I suppose, but I'm easily recognised as you can see." He gave a mocking gesture towards a birthmark on his face and he went silent, waiting for them to speak.

"What do you know about this man who hired you?" Josh demanded. "What did he look like?" He was trying to keep calm, but this was the nearest he had got to finding out who his enemy was. The questions were bubbling away inside of him, but he knew the man could not answer all of them. Best to get what he could out of him, Josh reasoned.

The man absentmindedly rubbed the glue from his face as he considered the questions Josh had asked. "He was a stranger in the town, just like me. I know that for a fact. Well-dressed, and looked like he had plenty of money. He gave me some money for expenses to get here, and I would get the rest in a parcel from Duloe when you were dead."

"How would he know when you had killed Josh? Did you have to tell him?" Amy asked, her voice sharp with anxiety.

"No, he said that he would know if I'd done the job. There was someone in Nowhere keeping an eye on Josh Barnes. When I asked him, he said this man would kill no one but kept him informed of your whereabouts."

Josh's face paled as the enormity of what the man had said sank home. But he put the thought aside. Later, he would think about it. "What did the man look like? What did he sound like? Can you tell me anything about the man?" Josh angrily asked the man, fearing that he was almost getting to the stage of pleading with him for information.

The man, still rubbing at his gluey face, looked Josh up and down and then shook his head. "He looked like you, even sounded like you. Like as two peas in a pod, you are!"

CHAPTER SIXTY

In the silence that seemed as loud as an actual thunderclap in the general store, the man thrust his money at Amy and grabbed his provisions. He opened the door, and shouted back at Amy and Josh. "I'm leaving this place. I'm going to San Francisco. Got a brother there. You've no need to fear me. But there's someone in Nowhere who is watching you, and sending reports back to your double, the man they call Duke. You'd best watch out for him!"

Josh followed the man to the door and watched as he sorted his provisions onto his horse, which was tied up to the hitching rail outside the general store. He gave a glance back at the store after he'd mounted his horse, saw Josh standing there, and gave him a farewell salute before turning his horse's head and heading out of Nowhere.

"Someone is watching you and selling information about you. Who can it be?" Amy had walked across the store to join Josh in the doorway. They both watched the man as he rode off out of sight, only the dust trail behind him showing where he had been. "Do you think he's telling the truth? Or was he just saying it to leave us wondering?"

Manuel entered the room from the back of the store to find them standing, still staring silently after the man. "What's wrong with you two?"

Josh still stood, unable to stop staring after the man. There was nothing to see, but he couldn't get the man's comments out of his head. He couldn't make sense of them, and somehow he felt even more threatened by them. He heard the murmur behind him of Amy's voice as she explained what had happened to Manuel. The outburst of disgust and anger from Manuel at Josh's life being threatened and the thought of a spy being present in Nowhere watching Josh with evil intentions made Josh smile.

"Thanks, Manuel, I appreciate that. I'd like to ring this so-called Duke's neck as well. But I can't get over what that guy said. He said we look alike. Seems like I've got a family member who looks like me, and is eager to see me dead!" Josh stood still for a moment, and when Manuel and Amy were about to speak, he put his hand up to them. "No more, please. I don't want to think about it or talk about it anymore today. Time enough to think about it later. I need a coffee! Is there any brewing, Manuel? Or shall I get a pot on the go?" He walked to the back of the store and busied himself with putting coffee on the stove. With Eliza remaining in bed with the baby, after the new parents' broken night with Isabel's crying, the coffee hadn't been organised as usual.

Behind his back, Manuel and Amy exchanged glances. Amy shrugged and went back to the accounts. She grimaced as she sat down at the small table. Manuel began sorting out the hardware he had ordered, and the candles and oil lamps that had arrived the other day but had not been unpacked with Eliza giving birth. Both of them busied themselves, but as they did so, they kept glancing back at Josh. The coffee was brewed, and he handed out the tin cups they used in the store. Conscious of their worried glances at him, Josh smiled at them both. "I don't want to think about it anymore. My mind is going round in circles. Let's leave it for now, can't we?"

The bell jangled as the door was pushed open and Charles Roberts walked in with a beaming smile. Amy bent over the accounts, her braids falling forward and obscuring her face, and she busied herself rustling papers and writing in the account book. Josh put his coffee down and strolled forward to the counter. It was left to Manuel to approach the man who was standing there smiling round at them all.

"Congratulations, Manuel! I hear you have a new baby girl. Give my best wishes to Eliza, and I'm pleased to hear both mother and baby are doing well. Congratulations to Miss Amy as well. I hear you acted successfully as a midwife. There are no limits to your talents, are there, my dear?"

Manuel beamed with pride, his dislike of the man being overcome by joy in his newly born daughter. Amy could no longer hide her head and turned round to give Charles a cool smile and a nod. She murmured her thanks but did not rise to greet the man.

"Terrible sad news about old man Thompson. If only he had sold to me earlier. It must have been in his mind that he was going to do so, because he wrote out that will, leaving the property to me. Manuel, I think you'll have to expand the general store because I'm going to be encouraging lots of people to move into Nowhere. Business will be booming for you." Manuel smiled at the man and readied the few provisions Charles required. The transaction took place and was concluded. Charles Roberts never looked at Josh, whereas Josh was staring at him fixedly.

The goodbyes were said between them all. Amy received a kiss blown from his beautifully manicured hands, and then Charles picked up his provisions and walked to the door. Before he finally walked through it, he turned and stared directly at Josh. "Delighted to see you looking so healthy, Josh. Let's hope you keep that way."

CHAPTER SIXTY-ONE

"It's him! That was as good as saying he was surprised to see you alive. He's the one that spying on you, Josh. What can we do? How can we stop him?" Amy jumped up so quickly from her chair that it fell on the floor. Heedless of the fallen chair, she rushed to the window of the store and, leaning over some barrels, she stared down the road after Charles.

Manuel walked slowly up behind her and, placing his hand on her shoulder, he gave it a gentle squeeze. "There's nothing we can do. He just hoped Josh was well and hoped he would stay that way. Just a harmless comment, Charles would say if we questioned him about it. Josh is powerless against the man. He can't call him out on his comment. Josh would be laughed at, and Charles would love to make him look a fool. Don't you agree, Josh?"

Josh gave a harsh, dry laugh. "So our man Charles thinks he's very clever. Let's make him think that, shall we? He may have had a cheap jibe at my expense just then. But what he didn't know about was our new knowledge. Our informer told us there was a spy living in Nowhere and sending reports back about me to my would-be killer. Charles didn't know that when he made his so-called pleasant, double-edged remark. He knew that when he said it, but he didn't realise that we also knew it! Now we know who the spy is. Our man Charles is someone to observe from this moment on. Manuel, can you check out the post he receives, find out where it comes from and possibly who sent it?" Josh folded his arms as he came up behind the other two and watched as Charles smiled and waved to everyone he met on Main

Street. "I think I am going to enjoy bringing that man to justice, if not only for myself but also for old man Thompson."

The day passed quickly. Both Manuel and Josh worked hard in the store. Amy, supplied with the occasional tin cup of coffee and, at lunchtime, some bread and cheese, worked on throughout the day on the accounts. In late afternoon, Eliza appeared in the store, and she took up her usual chores for the closing of the store.

"Are you sure you should be up, Eliza? Don't you want to rest some more?" Amy looked up from her accounts, worried that Eliza would do too much too soon.

"No, my dear, I have rested enough. Few women have a considerate husband like me, or friends who will take over their tasks after childbirth. Some women have to get straight up and go back to work on the farm. I was the lucky one, so thank you, my dears."

Amy watched as Manuel moved the heavier baskets for his wife and gave her a quick kiss as he did so. The couple worked well together. Manuel was happy to help in what was termed woman's work, if it saved his wife from any pain or distress. Amy's eyes clouded over with tears, as a memory of her parents working together with love and affection during their marriage, before her mother was so cruelly taken away, came into her mind.

It was time to close the store. The vegetables and other products that were past their best were shared between them. Previously, Amy would return to the Broken Horseshoe Ranch with an odd assortment, wondering how she might make a meal out of it. No longer did she have that worry. No matter what she took home, Tom would pounce on it eagerly and spread it all out on the table. The provisions he already had at the ranch that needed to be used up would be added to those on the table. In no time at all, a delicious meal would be on the table, with fragrant smells and tasty herbs livening up the plainest and oddest mixture of supplies.

"I told Eliza about Charles Roberts and that remark of his which echoed the information we got earlier from the man who was sent to kill you. I expect, when Charles Roberts realises, he has gone and that you are still very much alive, he will get into contact with Duke," Manuel said, as he began drawing down the blinds in the shop window. "That's what he's going to do. You're still alive and the would-be killer is gone without carrying out his task. If we watch carefully, maybe we'll see who Charles is going to contact?"

"Manuel, that makes sense! I never even thought of that. The next few days are vitally important, and we really must keep an eye on Charles Roberts. That will be made so much easier as all the posts and parcels come through you at the general store. And he doesn't know that we have been informed about him," Josh said, a sudden grin breaking out on his face as he looked at Manuel. For once, Josh did not feel so powerless. Now he knew more about the man seeking to kill him. He also knew how this man was getting information about him. And, thanks to Manuel, there was a plan to be put into action. "Maybe, just maybe, I'll finally find out who wants me dead, and why!"

CHAPTER SIXTY-TWO

On their way into the general store the next morning, Josh and Amy met the sheriff. They knew it was him from some distance away. Only one figure had that tall, thin silhouette, with the black coat flying behind him and riding the heavy black horse. He pulled up beside them as Amy told Bella to halt.

"I'm off to the Hobbs' place. I'm going to accompany Dora back to Nowhere. She told me to come back for her after a few days. Not looking forward to it at all. We've had no word, you know. They could all be dead by now or turned mad by this devil nonsense!" The sheriff shook his head, worry lines creasing his face, as he wondered what was going to await him at the Hobbs' ranch. This was mixed with the anger he felt about the gullible, superstitious people around him, and how they seemed eager to accept any nonsense. "No doubt I'll meet you all later. I hope it's with good news, but I am prepared for the worst possible outcome of this devil's business." Shaking his head, he rode off. The dark figure looked lonely and yet forbidding as he became silhouetted against the sun's rays.

"There is something more that is worrying our sheriff, isn't there?" Josh said thoughtfully, as he watched the Sheriff ride away.

"What do you mean?" Amy asked, puzzled by his remark.

"What do we know about our sheriff and part-time preacher? Really know about him, or his past? Nothing! No one knows anything about the man. Where does he come from? We never see any family members. Do we know if he has any family? He dresses all in black, from head to toe. Why? He even has a black horse. How many people would have a black horse to match their clothes? I don't know any, do you, Amy?" Josh, his eyes fixed on the man, shook his head. "Somehow, I think our Sheriff Lance Grey has a very interesting past, and I would love to know what it is."

"I wouldn't ask too many questions about the man. It's dangerous to ask questions about any man when you come out West. And I don't think it would be a good thing to annoy our sheriff. He is not a man to be trifled with," Amy thoughtfully replied.

They continued to the stable behind the general store, neither saying anything further. Thinking about the sheriff brought them no answers, but just highlighted how little they knew about the man and his background.

"Where's the sheriff off to? I saw you talking to him as he left town," Manuel said to them as they walked into the store.

"He's off to see Dora at the Hobbs' place. He promised to go back after a few days to see what was happening there," Amy replied. She hung her satchel on the chair beside the table, which was still covered in pieces of paper and the two accounts books. Her heart sank as she looked at the papers, but it seemed to be more in order after her efforts of yesterday. "How is Eliza? And the baby?"

"Eliza is fine, Amy, and the baby slept through the night." Eliza's voice behind Amy made her jump as she turned round to look at the woman coming towards her.

Amy was delighted to see her friend looking so rested and rushed towards her to hug her. "Eliza, you look so much better today."

"I'm fine, thank you. You've all given me a chance to

recover from the birth, and I am truly grateful for it. But I'm looking forward to getting back into action again, especially as Manuel has such big plans in the future."

"Future plans for the store, Manuel? I know you've been talking about it. Are you going to start soon?" Josh said, as he carried the provisions they had brought from Broken Horseshoe Ranch into the store. He gently placed the eggs on the counter, before he set baskets of sweetcorn, beans, and Chan's latest venture at growing tomatoes beside them.

"Seth is nearly finished with the saloon building. I'm going to take advantage of his know-how and contacts, and even his workmen, to build on the side of the store. It will be a hardware store." Excitement flooded the large Mexican's entire body, and he bounced a little on his toes. He flung his arms wide to show how large the new store would be, "and I'm having a large sign painted. It won't say general store, it will say Mercantile!"

Exclamations of how wonderful and exciting broke out from Josh and Amy. Manuel expected to hear such remarks from them, and they both loved the chubby Mexican and his kind-hearted generosity towards them. It was the least they could do to ensure his continued excitement and happiness in this venture. And they were excited to be present at this fresh development in the general store.

Manuel and Josh had only a few deliveries that day and returned to Nowhere in the early afternoon. Amy had worked all morning over the accounts, her fingers becoming stained with the ink. The cloth beside her showed the many inks blots it had absorbed.

"Amy, leave that paperwork. I cannot stand to see you slaving over it any more. Come and help me sort out vegetables that have gone past their best. You can take some home for yourself, and we will have the others," Eliza said.

It took no time at all for Amy to straighten her papers and close up the account books, but only after blotting the ink carefully, cleaning the nib, and laying out her working utensils ready for the morning. She dashed over to join Eliza and placed some of the older produce into the basket for her return to the ranch that evening.

The door opening with a sudden jerk had both women looking up, startled at the entrance of a tall man wearing tattered Confederate trousers and a sweat-stained jacket. His unshaven appearance had both women on high alert. Amy recognised him at once as the man who had held Josh and herself up in Lonesome Creek and shot Josh in the arm.

CHAPTER SIXTY-THREE

He walked up to the counter and began delving deep into a pocket in the tattered trousers with the stripe. Producing some gold and silver coins, he placed them on the counter. He stared at Eliza. "There's money. I want all these provisions." A long list was placed on the counter beside the money.

Eliza took the list and called out to Amy. "Coffee, flour, and beans, Amy, to start with. You'd best get some sacks to put them in."

Amy reached for the bags of provisions and the sacks and carefully placed the goods on the counter. Keeping one hand free to reach for her gun if it was needed, she watched the man closely. She had recognised him immediately, but she was grateful that his attention seemed to be wholly focused on the shopping list. Amy, although in front of the man, now realised that he didn't recognise her at all from Lonesome Creek. No longer was he riding the old burro. Amy could see a large buggy hitched up to the rail outside. The goods he was buying from the store were not simply for one man, these were supplies for a group of men.

"I will just get your change," Eliza said, reaching for the money to take it to the cashbox.

The man stared at her for a moment, then he grabbed his sack and gave a large honking laugh. "No need, lady. No need at all. Plenty of money where that came from!" And he was gone. Carrying both sacks out to the buggy, he placed them on it. As they watched him, he unhitched the horse and, without a backward glance, drove the buggy down Main Street and out of town.

Eliza looked at the coins on the counter. "There's far

too much money here. He needed quite a lot of change out of this lot. What should I do, Amy? Do you think it was stolen?"

Although it was early morning the next day, the heat was oppressive when Josh and Amy set off on the usual morning journey to Nowhere. It was a heat that sapped the energy, leaving them listless and eager to get into the cooler shade of the general store. Even Bella, the horse, plodded along at an increased speed. She, too, was finding the heat unpleasant. There was much to discuss about the new plans of Manuel's and how they would affect their lives and their work at the store. But neither of them felt inclined to discuss or even think about how they would cope or what they would do next to fit in with Manuel's grand plan. It was too hot and oppressive.

Bella rushed into the stable, desperate for a long drink of water, obviously relieved to be out of the sun. Josh and Amy climbed up the stairs and went into the general store. They were both eager for a drink.

"Good morning, Amy. I'm just finishing up today's display of fresh vegetables and produce. Can you see to the baby? I'm sure I heard her move around in her basket," Eliza called out from the front of the general store.

Amy needed no second bidding and went and picked up Isabel, who was beginning to cry. "Hush Isabel, your Ma won't be long." The tiny baby held in Amy's arms looked up at her for a moment, before wrinkling her nose, ready to cry. "Hush Isabel." Amy's voice was no longer calm and gentle. There was a decided note of panic creeping into it. She was used to David, the little Indian baby, who was much sturdier and bigger. This tiny little creature she held in her arms was almost frightening in its tiny size and vulnerability. The footsteps of Eliza coming behind her made Amy turn in relief and pass the baby over to her quickly. "She is lovely, but I think she's going to cry again."

Eliza laughed at Amy, especially at her panic-stricken face. "Don't worry, I'll take her now. She was good during the night, so I was up early and swept everything outside, and I readied everything in the store to leave you free to finish those accounts."

"Thank you," Amy said and trudged off back to the paperwork, which she was loathing. Amy would rather sweep the store than struggle over Manuel's slipshod accounting books.

It was lunchtime, and the sky darkened as the enormous clouds swept in, lightning flashing in the dark thunderheads that came rolling down from Devil's Mountain. A continuous rumbling of thunder echoed around the desert landscape and seemed to reverberate off the jagged peaks and the mountainous foothills. Those in the general store rushed to the windows. This was an unusual storm. Outside on Main Street, they could see people gathered in doorways and windows all looking out, especially up to the lofty peak of Devil's Mountain. Thunder boomed, the very earth shook, and the jagged forks of lightning struck the highest peak again and again. Then came the rain. It swept along the ground into horizontal streams; drops the size of the largest coins clattered on the roofs and boardwalk, splashing high as they did so. In seconds, Main Street was awash. Waterfalls appeared flowing across tin and board roofs and torrents poured down the tented roofs of those temporary properties with the false fronts.

In seconds, it was over. The black clouds rolled away,

and the sun came out. The heat of the ground and the warmth from the sun on the street had the boardwalks and the roofs steaming. Into this mistiness rode a figure, waving his rifle and shouting.

They tumbled out of the doorways, from where they had sheltered from the storm, into the muddy street and onto the boardwalks. The rider came closer, his shouts became easier to understand the closer he came. "I wounded him! I shot the Devil!" He sat panting on his horse as they rushed around him.

Josh was one of the first to reach him. He stood beside the man and his horse, which was soaked after coming through the heavy storm. He recognised him as the farmhand who worked at the ranch next to the Grangers' and Thompson's ranches. Red, that was his name; Josh remembered, because of the mop of red hair and the beard which straggled down onto his chest. This was the other ranch that had been plagued by devilish signs, noises, and lights.

It was Manuel who calmed the man down and made him slow down so that they could try to make sense of his excited speech.

"Last night it started again, wavering lights through the trees, the howls, and yells. But this time I was ready for it. I had climbed a tree and sat there with my rifle. I saw a figure coming over to the henhouse about to grab a chicken. I fired and hit the man because he gave a shriek and yelled, and then ran off to his horse and rode away. But I winged him. That shot hit him, and he shouted in pain. That was no devil, it was a man!"

Excited chatter broke out between the crowd. "Someone has been deliberately terrorising our ranch and old man Thompson's place. It was no devil and no supernatural being. It was a man. I should know because I shot him!" Red waved his rifle again in the air, cries of jubilation coming from the burly man. The rest of the crowd joined in, and in no time at all Red was off his horse and was escorted with much backslapping into the saloon.

"So all we do now is to look out for an injured man. It might well be a clue to who has been acting as the Devil," said Manuel as they returned to the general store.

Only a short while later, another commotion broke out in the Main Street of Nowhere. "Here is the sheriff, and he has Dora riding with him." A man who was about to enter the store opened the door, and he shouted the news to the customers and staff before running off to see what was happening. Everyone rushed out, eager to hear what had happened out at the Hobbs' place. There had been great anxiety as the inhabitants of the small township were frightened that they too would become infected by the devil's illness that had laid the whole of the Hobbs family incapacitated or near to death.

CHAPTER SIXTY-FOUR

"Dora is smiling! Look, she's waving happily at everyone."

As her buggy drew nearer, beside her, riding his black horse, the sheriff also had a slight smile on his face. Josh felt the sheriff's unusual expression showed a great relief deep within the man because he'd never seen him smile at all before!

"Dora, what's happened? Are they all dead? What happened to those mad girls?" The anxious questions came from everyone and all sides. Dora drew her buggy to a halt beside the hitching rail in front of the general store.

It was the sheriff who took charge. "All is well in the Hobbs' place," he shouted out to the gathering crowd. Murmurs and chatter came from the crowd. Their relief was mixed with delight and the need for answers.

"Quiet, let Dora speak," the sheriff shouted at them all.

"They were poisoned! Special grain sent from relatives had been stored badly, but they used it anyway. I heard about this happening to another family back East. When it gets mouldy, it causes fits and visions and a constant jerking of limbs and dancing. We threw it out, and they are all getting better now," Dora shouted the news, broadcasting it to the crowd assembled around the buggy. "There was no devil at the Hobbs' place. It was a special poisoning called Ergot from the grain. No devil was ever there."

"But those girls said their father was the Devil, they said he was evil," said one matronly woman with her arms folded. A few heads nodded beside her. Some of the crowds were unwilling to let go of the devil's theory. It was more exciting than just bad grain.

The sheriff waved his arms again for silence. "That's enough. Settle down everybody. Red just told me he shot a man last night painting the devil signs on a barn door. There is no devil making signs, killing hens and wandering about with lights. Do you hear me? There was no devil at old man Thompson's place. It was a man seeking to frighten him. There is no devil at the Hobbs' place, that was just mouldy grain. So go back to what you were doing, sure of the fact that there is no devil in Nowhere!"

The crowd dispersed, muttering and mumbling. Some were highly delighted, and the relief was clear in their smiling faces. Others, regretfully, had to let go of the excitement which having the Devil in their midst had brought into their dreary lives.

"Eliza! You've had the baby!" Dora jumped off the buggy and rushed to see Eliza, who had come out onto the boardwalk. Dora looked her up and down. "How did you manage? I see you're looking well, and the baby? What did you have? Is the child healthy?" Eliza replied with nods and smiles as the questions came at her fast from Dora. "Who helped you?" Dora whirled around to the smiling Amy standing on the boardwalk watching this conversation with interest.

"Amy helped me. Isabel came quickly and easily. I was blessed to have an easy birth, Dora. And Amy was a wonderful help throughout it all," Eliza said, putting an arm around the girl.

"Don't keep me standing here! I want to see the baby!" Dora and Eliza went off to look at the sleeping baby.

Josh had been standing with a rather peculiar expression on his face. "Amy, come here and look. Manuel, look at who I see with his arm in a sling. He seems to have been injured. I wonder how he got his injury?"

The indrawn breath from Amy and the muttered cursing from Manuel showed that they, too, had reached the same conclusion as Josh. Walking down the main street was Charles Roberts with his arm in a sling. "Charles Roberts has been the man acting as the Devil. Surely, he will finish those antics now. It's been proved not to be the work of the Devil at the Hobbs' place and the Thompson ranch. It must have been him the whole time, trying to drive out the ranch owners, forcing them to sell their properties at a cheap price for the fear of the Devil."

"Behind that smile of his, there is an evil man," Amy said, watching Charles walking down the street and smiling as he shook hands with all that he met. His remaining good hand.

"Thank goodness, everything has worked out for the best. All the devil signs and mutilated chickens will cease, and the Hobbs' place is now free from illness and visions of the Devil. Now they are all healthy, and nowhere can become a peaceful town once again," Manuel said and sighed in satisfaction as he turned to go into the general store.

Before he could open the door, shouts came from the end of Main Street. The wagon from Duloe raced down Main Street at an unusually fast speed. Manuel turned back and rushed towards the hitching rail beside Josh and Amy, who had turned to watch this unexpected occurrence. The normally surly, taciturn driver began waving to Manuel as he drew up outside the general store and shouted at the top of his voice. "It's Jesse James! He's robbed a train and a bank and is on his way here. We saw him and his gang up at the top of the ridge yonder. Jesse James is coming to Nowhere!"

About The Author

Janey Clarke writes charming, witty, cosy mysteries. From septuagenarian shenanigans in Cornwall to the intrigue of Regency-era whodunits and now to her newest venture into the rugged drama of the Wild West. When not plotting her next twist or researching historical details, she can be found exploring the stunning Jurassic Coast in Dorset with her loyal spaniel by her side. With a passion for tea, old books, and well-timed humour, Janey Clarke creates stories she hopes will whisk readers away to delightful worlds where solving a mystery is always the order of the day. And always solved by a feisty heroine! Visit Janey at www.janeyclarke.com to learn more about her books.

www.blossomspringpublishing.com

Made in the USA
Columbia, SC
10 April 2025

56443665R00155